Northern Guard

ZORAN MASLIC

ISBN-10:0994855109
ISBN-13:9780994855107

DEDICATION

This book belongs to the genre of science fiction, but it is based on real life events even though it was written much before they would happen. I dedicate it to all my comrades from guardian duty.

CONTENTS

"I've recorded everything with a red pen!"

Stanislaus Kos,

High Interrogator of the Republic

1 THE ORIGIN OF SPECIES

She told me this:

Hey! Hey! Hey! It cannot be forgotten. Nobody can ever forget it! There are no chains or bars that can stop me! Listen, and remember! I'm not going to say it twice. Forget your machines! They're just broken coffee grinders, can openers! Check it out! They cannot grab my words because I have skills. I know how to walk through the minefield of mind! Don't be scared! Come on in under the shadow of this rock. I will show you your fear. I'm just joking; testing you. I see, you don't know much about the old culture. Yeah, write if you wish! Actually, I like it.

You're so sure that you're an inspector, a scientist, that you have the knowledge, but if somebody destroyed your database, you'd be lost. The brain is a labyrinth, just like the universe. And you, what did you do with it? You reduced it to a living room and bedrooms, to kitchen and closets and balconies! Your labyrinths "evolved" into dead matter because you were strong, you lazy victors. Your ancestors never deserved this planet. They were as primitive as those on the Earth when one Human would be a slave to another, like a domestic animal. Cheap! Cheap! Cheap!

Your founding fathers wanted Cheap! They were happy with the "natural obedience" of dogs and they thought, if we mix these genes with Human genes we will produce a skillful and submissive creature that will work for nothing! Lowlifes! They enjoyed throwing a bone into the dust to somebody faithful!

And here we are, neither Humans nor dogs! Sometimes I hate that side of myself. Your side! I will never understand why you would do something like that. How could you do it to yourself? There is you in me and there is no me in you. I can laugh and I can cry thinking of that. You are bored? OK, I will talk. I will tell you everything, but when I am done you might realize why I would. It will be late for you. Let's start at the beginning.

Seventeen: an age when a girl dreams of her rosy future. Well, it wasn't like that for me! Industrious, but futile, were the efforts of my mother to shape me into a lady who would attract some groom from high society. Unfortunately, I was just a tomboy, always ready for a fight. I must have looked funny in those silk 'n' lace dresses she forced me to wear when somebody visited. My girlfriends were having experiences parents didn't know about, but I was still "illiterate" that way. Seventeen, the age of blurry resistance! My father, he defined me. He was seeing in me both his daughter and his son, and he often treated me as a boy. He enjoyed my mischievous deeds, silently approved of my street fights, and he just laughed when he found a slingshot, a set of brass knuckles, and a pack of cigarettes in my school bag. It drove my mother crazy. Even guys at school called me Miller-Killer, after that character from the TV series. Simply, I was not born for the stupidities that usually occupy the brain of a teenage girl. I guess I wanted to become somebody in the world of men. I was also a classroom clown. "But a good student!" my father would add.

I was the informal leader of a pack of tough-guy wannabes. We thought we were a gang and we had a cool name — The Dragons. They would probably have kicked me out of the school long ago if my family hadn't been one of the most prestigious among the dog population of Chortwille. As you know, my grandfather, Vasiliy Aganovski, was the Dog's High Commissioner of the city, and my father Konstantin ran a factory of twenty thousand workers that produced food exclusively for Humans. At the age of five, my brother Andrey was sent to Military School to become an Officer of the Guard of the Republic, which is something not everybody can dream about.

So, I led a double life. On the street I was a guy dressed in black leather with all those chains and stuff. At home, I had to be an upper-class cutie who played piano in her antiseptic dresses, in the dreamy afternoons, when the light declines and parents take tea. But enough about old me. This is how it started.

The maids were finishing up the cleaning. All sorts of good smells were wafting from the kitchen. Mum was running up and down, fussing constantly and giving new instructions: the curtains should be opened wider, put roses on that corner table, bring more logs for the fireplace, more pineapple in the cake, the honey for that baklava shouldn't be too thin, but not too thick either! Father was in his favorite armchair, reading Democracy Star and listening to my attempts to play piano pieces by Shultz-Remizov and Libanowsky. For us, that day was bigger than the Day of the Republic or New Year's Eve because Andrey was coming. When he appeared in the door I was to commence with "The Ode of Joy," the old servant Sam was to toss confetti, our chef was supposed to present him with a plate full of specialties and father would uncork the Champagne bottle and spray the returnee.

Instead, we waited. And waited. And we waited again.

And the phone rang. A deep masculine voice said that

Andrey would not come home, but that everything was fine. We should not worry. He didn't come that day or the day after. He showed up two months later, unannounced, sunburnt, skinny, wrapped in a desert toga. He'd brought a friend, similar to him, but with a scar on his cheekbone. I went weak in my knees. I was meeting my brother for the first time! I'd only ever seen him in photos. I surprised myself by crying, just like an ordinary spoiled girl who didn't get her favorite treat: schneenockerl. Andrey hugged me.

"Anyushka, oh Anyushka!" he said.

I could only respond, "Oh, Andrey!" Mother appeared at the living room door. She screamed, embracing her son desperately. Soon we were having tea.

Andrey asked about Dad and his job, about my school, and many other things, yet said nothing about himself. His friend was quiet; he would give short answers and smile politely. His name was Mrako Pravica, and he shared a room with Andrey at the Academy. Mother seemed to be upset with their looks, but she hid it. You could see that life was whipping them.

The dinner had already started when father came. He had trouble hiding his confusion, but he quickly pulled himself together and the rest of the day behaved as though Andrey had never been absent. Mother was recalling funny events from Andrey's early childhood and we all laughed. Suddenly, Andrey turned dead serious and stared into father's eyes. "You know what's going on?" Dad just nodded.

Mother knew something wasn't right. "What's going on?"

"The war," said father.

"With who?"

"With the Arijaans."

"With the Humans!" said Andrey.

Father looked at him, surprised.

"But how?" said Mom. "Nothing is really happening."

"Arijaans, the desert dogs. It is still a secret, but you'll hear about it soon," whispered Andrey.

"Oh, those poor fools," whined mother. "They don't stand a chance. Humans are so mighty!"

Leaning forward, Mrako coughed, and said in a low voice, "My dear lady, the Humans aren't dealing with them. We're the ones who fight. The only ones that will suffer in this war will be the dogs! And the Humans? They'll watch it on TV. That's why we're here now. Andrey and I are part of the guard that will raise the alarm in the fighting sector in the case of attack. Once that's over, we'll graduate from the Academy and become lieutenants. I hope that'll be in two or three months."

"That is a great honor," said my mother.

Father was looking at his shoes.

2 WHAT HAPPENED IN RABBAT

The Institute for Climate Support announced the coming of Spring, an event that always filled me with excitement. I could see from my room the trees in the garden beginning to bud. A mild wind would caress my face, and suffuse my nostrils with the promise of Summer. Normally, I would put skates on my feet and the switchblade in my pocket and the streets of Chortwille would be mine. Today, I wasn't in the mood. Instead, I slipped into my new violet dress, black shoes, gloves, and hat. Insecure at first, fearing that somebody might laugh at me, I chose streets where I didn't expect to see known faces. Still, Dizzy, a prick from school, saw me. His ironic eyes made me want to smash his face to a pulp, but I just passed by, pretending to look at shop windows. With every step my anxiety was shrinking, the dress was becoming part of me. I felt my inner thighs rub together, my hips becoming heavy. Three boxers and a Bull Mastiff took my measure with their eyes. I found some pleasure in it.

I was going to Rabbat, the entertainment ghetto. I never had the courage to do it, not even with my Dragons. All the stories about Rabbat seemed to be true. First, you go through a system of narrow passages with plastic mirror-walls all around you. No vehicle could get through. The entrances are the size of ordinary doors, no higher than 1.4 meter, which means that Humans, normally double that size, couldn't get in. Certainly, if any of them wanted to, they could find a way, but nobody remembers such a thing ever happening.

Shock is the first thing you get. Lights are flashing everywhere; the streets feel like the halls of a house in which a wild party is taking place. Hookers in black and red plastic skirts constantly drop their handkerchiefs and stoop to pick them up. The street food consists of tortillas, pizza, chevapi, burek. There are hundreds of restaurants, sex shops, theatres, carnival-sized crowds, lumberjacks showering in beer, blue- collar workers haggling with whores about prices, faggots in public bathrooms, junkies sticking needles in their veins in plain sight. I bought piroshky and cautiously moved through this anthill.

A black shop window caught my eye. It seemed more like a funeral home, but its gold letters announced Discotheque Morning Star. I entered. A jester in black appeared before me, his crazed eyes glaring through dark bags. He bowed, and then fell on his knees theatrically, like in some kind of opera.

"Oh, please, come on in, my princess! Please, bless this modest place of honest and God-fearing folk. You look so cute biting into that piroshky! And the ticket is just five dinars, less than a membership of a library or a minimum donation to a charity!

I barely had money out of my purse when he grabbed it, bowed, and rushed down the hall. Music was shaking the walls. Black Jester pressed some buttons on the remote control and one wall suddenly opened, exposing a vending machine that blinked like an ancient pinball machine. It was filled with the latest synthetic drugs. I bought a pack of Ithaca Hash, v. 5.7. The floor opened, revealing steep spiral stairs similar to Earth's mosque minarets. I descended some twenty meters into the boiling stomach of the Morning Star. Strange-looking dogs danced in stroboscopic light. They all wore black suits and made jerking motions with their torsos while their hands waved like they were sewn on. Their heads were hitting something invisible, the sweat was pouring down their stiff necks. The stairs ended in the center of the dance floor. From the moment you arrived you were treated like a star. Girls looked almost the same as guys; those with long hair had it tied, and all wore the same undertaker suits.

A waiter took my hand. "Come, my dear, I know how you feel." We went to a costume-storage and I hastily donned an undertaker costume. I chose a table close to the bar, determined to have my pack of sinthy. Less visible now, I smoked with confidence. Suddenly, I felt my nipples get stiff under the shirt, the lighting gradually faded, and the whole place almost imperceptibly sank into reddish darkness. Before I knew it, a Dogo with icy-blue eyes was sitting next to me, pouring a cognac.

"Beautiful place!" he said.

"It's not bad," I replied, acting cool, but he wasn't fooled.

"No offence intended, but you are a bit excited. I can smell from here that you are getting slippery between your legs!" he laughed cynically.

I slipped on my brass knuckle-duster and punched his filthy mouth. His teeth smashed like an ice-cube falling on a marble floor. Quickly, I was surrounded by five or six dogs. Bloody Rabbat! Did I lose my mind here? I was neck deep in shit without even knowing how I got there. I pulled out my switchblade with its electric shocker. They circled around me as though performing some ritual dance. They laughed, the creeps. I tried to cover my back. The other customers moved away slightly, but continued dancing, totally unfazed. This place had its own rules. Time was against me. I attacked the closest one, but a swift blow to the back of the skull felled me. The music had changed. I floated on the waves of a Shultz-Biederholf étude, naked, lying on a concrete runaway.

Sunset. Our Big and Small Sun were fading in this cosmic colon we call the world. Like in porn cartoons, satanic laughter echoed in this newly created vacuum. I opened my eyes: dogs were screaming with glee, ripping off my clothes, and groping me with their glue-like hands. Idiotic mirror balls swung evenly while the voice from the speakers sang:

I'll gnaw your bones, baby
If you ever enter my caddy,
Oh, I'd lick all of you,
If only you'd say YES.

I fidgeted helplessly, and wept, like a kid punished for something it didn't do. The circle of my captors opened and I realized with horror that shuffling towards me was one of those illegal experiments of genetic engineering: a rat as big as a pig, with a swollen penis sticking out of its forehead. Why the hell did I come here?!

I closed my eyes, froze. Waited. I wished I were dead. Time stopped. I saw my parents crying over my mutilated body in a morgue. Suddenly I heard, "Get up, honey! It's OK!" Above me was a dog with black sunglasses, pulling me up. Those bullies were lying all over the place, dead as squirrels on an autobahn. The dog took off his glasses. He smiled. It was Mrako, Andrey's friend.

She will be seventeen just this June,
She has nobody to tell her, to tell her,
"You are mine! You are mine, you are!"
from the song She Is Waking Up by Sharlo Akrobata

9

3 IN THE CAR

The engine of our black Boa purrs perfectly. We're driving through Chortville. I'm calm, sipping tonic-vodka. I want that car to glide forever. At moments, Mrako looks disturbed, even foolish. Neon commercials are reflecting on his sweaty face. Is it possible that the Rabbat event had upset him more than me? I don't think so. I keep asking questions, and the answers are always the same. "Your brother is well," or "It's not bad where we are," or "We'll celebrate the promotion together."

"Will your parents come?" I ask.

"No."

"They can't, or...?"

"I really don't want to talk about that! OK?" Then silence. We are already passing the shiny windows of the Golden Charshia, the merchants' quarter.

"I feel that you want something from me."

"That's true."

"OK?"

"I don't know..."

"You don't know what? Listen, I do appreciate that you saved me, but don't lie to me! What's going on with

10

Andrey?"

"I think it's best if I drive you home."

"Huh! Future officer of the Guard! No time for talking with kids! I demand an explanation! Why don't we hear from my brother? Supposedly, you can't leave the camp! Then I see you having fun in Rabbat! And acting like a gentleman!"

"Anya, your brother and me... Your brother is in danger!" His response surprised me. I had expected him to say that he had temporarily slipped away in search of whores, or booze, or whatever.

"You know that we are part of the Guard of this city. Andrey left tonight, but hasn't come back. If they ever found out, they'd hunt him down. And his chances would be slim. I was simply searching for him; I don't know... maybe I was even looking for some kind of replacement. I guess it was stupid not to tell you."

"What the hell are you talking about?"

"Well, it's a long story. Andrey doesn't know that he's not covered. I was supposed to pick up his replacement tonight, in the Morning Star. It went all wrong. The replacement is gone. I actually met the guy and we were about to leave when he went to bathroom. He never came back. I found his body on the toilet. And what do you think was in the toilet? What, Anyushka? His head! His damn head! Then I saw you! Everything else you know."

"Are you insane?"

"God sent you!"

"Hello? Are you hearing me?"

"I'm telling you the truth, Anya."

"Why do you think that Andrey would be in deep shit?"

"I can't tell you that. I guess you don't know how military discipline works."

"OK. Why it is dangerous for you?"

"I'm the commander of the Northern Guard."

"Do you have a phone?"

"No."

"Stop there! Do you have a coin?" He had a special-edition coin, the one with the White Angel. Some save them for good luck. It fell in the belly of a dirty pay phone.

"Hello! Dad! Yes, it's me. I am so sorry I cannot explain. But it's nothing to worry about. No, everything is good...Look, dad, I can't come home tonight...It is something serious, but everything is fine. I don't know when... You'll have to trust what I say. I love you."

Beeep...

A long, nauseating argument with Mrako culminated with me agreeing to cover for Andrey. He still avoided telling me where my brother was. Everything was on a need-to-know basis, that was what was "best for me", for him, and for Andrey. Then he admits that he counted on me. We leave our car in Acid Varosh and enter a ruined house with no roof. Everything was like in a movie. The occasional dried turd told me that the place was not completely abandoned. He pulled out some bricks and from "the secret chamber" removed military clothing. He cut my hair. We turned our backs to each other and put our uniforms on.

"You look pretty much like Andrey, except he's taller."

I didn't say anything. I thought it was all crap, but essentially I believed in his good intentions. We walked for a while and then crawled through the tunnel that was going under barbed wire and mine fields. When we went out we were in a different world: the Guard Zone.

Kidneys remember the Watch,
Your courage depends on scotch,
Everyone is telling you, "Die!"
For you, no one will cry!

4 GUARDS' NIGHTS

An intense cold ruled over the guarded space or the "tampon," between the desert and the city. The Institute boasted in the media about this latest achievement. While sunny spring twittered in Chortville, the Zone was exposed to the archaic cold of the mother planet. The change was so sudden that you had to learn how to enter or exit the zone, how to put on or remove clothes, at what speed you should move. You actually see the wall of cold or heat wavering. It was very helpful. The Institute was intensely researching how to fix this flow. It was assumed that despite our having the enter-exit technique, Arijaans would figure it out. The "surprise effect" would be lost. Surprise? What kind of surprise it is if you hear about it everywhere? It took quite some time just to enter or exit. We called it the Frozen Hot Dog Dance. Essentially, you had to move all the time and kind of jiggle between zones for a while, gradually decreasing your time in one and increasing the time in another one. If you just tried to walk in, like you would walk through any normal gate, you'd die from an heart attack. I could not understand why the government would freeze its own soldiers, but... whatever!

Mrako pulled two grey-green coats from a low frozen bush. We put them on swiftly. In its inside pocket was a brand new customizable Stepa 68 automatic rifle waiting for me. He explained to me how to operate it. It was simple. We had to go. I followed. The night was beautiful. The freezing air hurt my lungs, but the abundant moonlight and glittering stars made me forget about it. We moved carefully between trees and through bushes to finally stop in front of a small artificial hill. There was something like a shack hidden in a moon shadow, more like a house that had sank into the soil, but only to hide its real purpose.

Somebody yelled from the dark, "Glorious is our path!"

"Lonely are the brave!" Mrako replied. A weak light appeared on the dark hill: there was a silhouette in the door frame. We went in.

"Is everything OK?" said Mrako.

"Yes. We just escorted the second shift. Everybody else is sleeping. So you got him to cover for Andrey?" the stranger whispered, looking around cautiously.

"You can call him Andrey," Mrako said, laughing.

"Hi! I'm Emil, Lance Corporal Emil. You'll be at Nine. That's one of the tougher security spots. I recommend that you go to sleep immediately. Your shift is in three hours. Other soldiers arrived just yesterday, they're all new. No reason to fear anything — they barely know each other. When on guardian duty, think only of your own security and the eventual arrival of a control officer. Focus on them alone and you'll be fine." He opened the bedroom and showed me my bed. It stank of sweat, dirty socks, and soldiers' rotten teeth.

I lay with my clothes on, resting my head on my own hand. The pillow was greasy. I pretended to sleep, but I was really just listening, trying to adjust to the place. In the hall, Emil and Mrako chatted loudly, they were probably drinking. They laughed like they were having a good time in some shady lower-class pub. I thought of my parents. Will they think that I ran away with some dog, or that I was partying somewhere? Drugged? Raped? Who knew what kind of thoughts were going through their heads now. They might be already withdrawing money from the bank, hoping that all of this is about a ransom; they must be waiting for the phone to ring. Minutes will stretch like years and no news will come. Nobody, friends, the school, the police, will know a thing. All those questions and guesses melted inside me, merged into a choking feeling of despair.

And then, the door opened with the bang. The lights turned on, strong, almost painful.

"First Shift, get up! Get the fuck up! What are we waiting for? Faster! Move your fucking asses!" screamed Lance Corporal Emil while hitting the metal railings of beds with his baton. Some soldiers had slept in their uniforms and boots and you could see how advantageous that could be. Others were sleepily putting their clothes on, mumbling curses. Emil was cruising through the aisles like a killer bee, tirelessly repeating this mantra, "Get up! Get up! Get your fucking asses up, you bunch of masturbating lesbian snails!" I waited in the hall trying to imitate the way others put their equipment on. I felt no fear, but I was confused. We walked in a squad-file formation to the battlement . It was at the side of the building.

"Shift, on the line now!"

"Rifles on the wall!"

"Unlock!"

"Ready!"

"One by one, FIRE into the earthwork!"

"Lock!"

"Receive ammunition!"

"On your right shoulder!" Suddenly he didn't yell anymore but whispered in a friendly fashion. "Challenge— LIQUIDATION! The password is FAWN!" Then he screamed again, "Shift, in a file squad column, follow me!"

We walked towards the dome of yellow light made by

the helico-transporter. It was just a little cockpit for three persons and an iron cage for soldiers pathetically covered with camouflage canvas. As soon as we piled inside the cage, the aircraft took off violently. We jumped around inside rather than sat. I started to understand that the army, stiff and cruel, with no consideration of civilization's achievements and standards of comfort, so normal in everyday life, would stick to its rough ways. The wind was awful. We could see inside of the warm cockpit through the little window on the back. It looked like they had a great time in there seeing us frozen, the helico would occasionally land and Emil would yell through loudspeakers the number of the guard spot. The new guardian would jump out, the old one would jump on. My turn came. "Nine! Number fucking nine! C'mon! What are we waiting for! The shift is late!" The old guardian hastily passed me the phone and before I knew it the helico had flown away.

A grave silence.

Panic hit me like a gusting wind. I tried to unlock my rifle. Thinking the gloves prevented me, I stupidly removed them and my skin stuck to the cold metal. I unlocked it somehow.

Through fields, coming from the West like a lion on the hunt the fog was approaching slowly. Judging by the reeds and some other plants, I concluded that this had been a marshy area some time ago. Life here had stopped, waiting for better days.... There was a strip of forest stroked by torn bushes on the other side. Its dark presence made me feel extremely uncomfortable. The fog was already swallowing me. I could feel it on my face, the fog of the Zone that bites and gets stuck to your skin and clothes. What kind of bloody fog is this? I did not even know if fog is supposed to be possible in that cold. I buttoned my greasy coat and squatted instinctively.

My phone hissed. Only the phone and the rifle had modern touches. For example, the phone was able to imitate the sounds of the environment you were in.

"Hello!"

"Hello? What the hell! You don't say hello! You say Guardian spot number whatever, guardian on duty, Ivan Ivanovich, Nino Ninich, Santa Claus, whatever your name is!"

"I understand!"

"Is it spot Nine?"

"Yes, sir!"

"Guard Commander talking. I'll be there in five minutes. Don't stop us! Over."

I grabbed my rifle and pointed it towards the reeds. Through the scope you could see everything. I thought I saw a silhouette of somebody running behind reeds, but didn't have time to get scared for the helico suddenly roared from the other side. Mrako walked out. He stood waiting for me. I signaled from the bushes. He waved to the pilot and the helico left.

"You scared?"

"Nope."

"You are lying, Anya, but that's OK!"

"This is all so sudden and different..."

"I know."

For a moment he disappeared in a fog. He was unshaven, with short but messy hair, his face swollen from booze and lack of sleep. Still, his very presence had a calming effect. Some fifty meters away something was breaking frozen bushes. I pointed my rifle there, but he just laughed like nothing had happened.

"Chill out! Those are jumping porcupines. In winter, they come to marshlands. For them, this is like a freezer full of food. They are confused; they think it is winter now. They will attack you only when they think that you are attacking them... I know how you feel. Events are zipping by like race cars and you feel you can't catch up. But, you never know! Maybe this was the choice your destiny made for you. It certainly chose you and pushed you on the path you must walk on. Don't be afraid."

"Don't you think that you owe me an explanation?" He said nothing.

"Did you lie to me? Where is my brother?"

"He's safe."

"And that's all you have to tell me?"

"Pretty much."

"Go to hell!"

"Anya, there is a reason for all of this."

"Is he alive?"

"I said that he is safe! Even if I could tell you more, you wouldn't understand."

"Why? I am not mature enough?"

"Anya, I swear on my life that I am telling you what is best for your brother, for you, for everybody." He put his hand on my arm, his eyes pleading for my trust.

"When will I know the truth?"

"I can't say, but I sure hope it will be soon."

He made me believe him, offered me a cigarette. We hid in bushes, masking our smokes with our palms. He talked and talked: about patience, about the rules of guard duty, the officers who would be checking up on you, the ways they went about it, about the Control Officer whose visit to guardian base was like the Third Coming of God, about the cold and how to stay warm, how to sleep safely and to never get caught. He showed me a dugout some soldiers had made long ago. It was a secret, a dangerous one.

I was strangely calm when the helico came back and Mrako went away.

A field mouse is tiny,
Yet when you hear him
Running at night,
You're jealous, guardian.

He runs to his Love
Where nights are hot!
He is going somewhere
Where you cannot!

5 ESCAPE TO THE CITY

Friday afternoon. Ismail, the guardian from my shift, is telling me I am a fool.

"Your skull will freeze! Engineers from the Institute drive temperatures to -45!"

"So what?! I like it this way! Just shave."

And Ismail shaved me. My hair was falling on the clean sheet: locks of rust. My scalp was showing as white as a cigarette rolling paper, like a dead man's skin. I don't know how to explain the joy I felt in making myself ugly. An old song from Raven's Feather's first album came to my mind.

TO·THE MAINLAND

On hot afternoon
I rode into a town
where a hammer was pounding nails,
industrious and calm.

I fell into the saloon
and skinned-mice sea

formed in the raft,
into a picture of my Lady.

She is pounding nails,
industrious and calm,
Oh, she's pounding nails,
industrious and calm.

Then, the divine voice tells me,
"With corpses mark your path!
On this mission of Light
may blessed be your wrath."

Understanding nothing,
I raise my cross high,
following the rhythm
"To the mainland!" I cry.

I looked at myself in the mirror. I felt an urge to take Ismail's blade and make a cut across my face, to have my teeth taken out and then laugh like a lunatic at upper-crust parties! Mrako arrived.

"Hmm. There are certain truths you can see only if you get rid of acceptable codes. That's the way to test the world!"

"Quite smart for a guard commander!"

He smiled, "You wanna be a tough guy?"

"It's my fifth day on duty."

He understood what I wanted to say, "Your brother is fine. He will call soon." We went out to have a smoke. I was exhausted by cold and sleepless nights. Every minute was precious — time you could use for sleep. Still, I wanted to talk with him.

"Tonight, we are going to the city," said Mrako.

"You are not afraid?"

"No. I am covered."

"Who's covering for you?"

"It doesn't matter. The point is: you can go with me."

"Where?"

"Rabbat! Where else?!"

"Sure. When?"

"Between 7 and 11. Then you can make it on time for your shift."

We left the Zone by the same way we came in. We put civilian clothes on and in a poor suburb of Kula we took a cab. I thought I would cry when I saw the city, it felt like a thousand years had passed since I was there.

"You miss your home?"

"Yes."

"Call your family."

We walked into the bar called Discarded Reasons. On the screen, a huge Bulldog was using and abusing a Poodle. The audience was shady. The waiter brought us a small bottle of glow-vodka even though we never ordered it. Mrako pulled out his new toy, a supposedly safe phone.

"Hello? Aganovski residence?"

"Oh my God! It's you, Anyushka! How are you, my dear? When are you coming home?"

Father was full of questions. I couldn't say much more than "Don't worry... blah-blah." Then mother cried, "Forgive us, Anyushka. Mom and Dad didn't mean, didn't want... Forgive everything! Come home!"

"But Mom, I am not angry at you. You see, if I didn't leave, something horrible would have happened! I love you, Mom! I'll be back... but not soon. Believe me, Mom... I love you!"

"Let's go! I said to Mrako." He handed me a bottle.

"We're going nowhere. We have to wait."

The bulldog was heartily working on the poodle and others were offering themselves from the front. She was squealing and moaning and when it looked like she'd get to the top the velvet curtains opened and a muscled mastiff stepped in. With a silver axe, he cut off her head. I lost my breath, my stomach contracted. What a place!

"Be calm! You're the man! We don't want to draw any attention." This sick combination of bar, movie theatre, junkie shop, and sadist's club could exist only in Rabbat.

The waiter approached us again, "The gentleman you're waiting for is at the bar now. Should I tell him to come over?"

Mrako nodded. The mysterious stranger looked just like mysterious strangers from bad movies, like he was afraid he might disappoint us with a lack of theatrical secrecy. And sure, he had sunglasses in the dead of night, his eyes invisible. He had shaken hands with Mrako and sat down without even glancing at me or showing any sign that he noticed my presence.

From a tiny jar he took some stardust and made a thin line on the table. He offered Mrako a little paper tube, Mrako sniffed and momentarily his head went up like it got filled with helium. He did the same as Mrako. Then, the stranger offered some to me.

Fellatio and Beathaven's "Erotica" was in the movie. The dogs from the bar actually looked worse than those on the screen...and then — IT! Like a spontaneous combustion, the "flame" spread inside me, my soul went up and reshaped into a Condor. I was gliding through the heavenly blue. Every sound was echoing in my head while I was looking from above on waving rye fields. It all sounds pathetic, but it was actually very different as a real experience.

It seemed that in the space between my ears, inside my very skull, was a radio receiver that made me listen to some conversation. Sometimes it was very clear, sometimes with lots of noise and interference.

"Did you initiate her?"

"No."

"Why?"

"I wasn't sure how she'd take it."

"You have to do it!"

"You do it!"

Two other Condors were flying next to me. The long sand beach was below us. They continued their radio talk.

"What's down there?" said the first Condor.

"It's the shore of all words that were ever pronounced: fake promises, dashed hopes, definitions, curses, utterances of love..."

"Hmmm. But I see nothing but an ordinary beach! Young men are playing volleyball, a beauty is tanning, a bodybuilder is surfing like it's an exhibition, there is a white sail on the open sea..."

"Sure. You might be right. You see things as you think they should be, but if you would really see, you'd see a shore of rusty iron letters that can cut your feet."

I had wanted to interrupt, but I couldn't make any sound. It felt like first condor was actually asking questions instead of me.

"Are you trying to say that what I see does not exist?"

"No, the thing is that what you see has thousands of ways not only to be seen, but to manifest itself. Look again!"

"You're right. The sea is red. From rust?"

"Or from blood!"

"From blood?!"

"From the blood that is to be shed!"

"Why are you playing with me? This is not a sanatorium! You're not a doctor!"

"You're wrong. I am just bringing you into an assignment. I want to heal you so one day you can ride the waves or sail on the open sea."

"I don't understand! Let's just land!"

"That's not an option. It's you who would suffer."

"Me?"

"You don't know how to walk."

"Your answers drive me insane."

"When you are insane enough you will be born."

"I'm going down! I'm not a bird! I want to walk!"

"Maybe you could walk, but you wouldn't know what you were stepping on."

"I would be stepping on sand that I can see."

"Or on dusty iron letters as sharp as military daggers. You could cut your foot on L; D is a trap for one leg, B for both. V could be a boomerang, if you threw it."

"Who are we?"

"We are birds that will burn."

Suddenly there was an explosion. The detonation threw me somewhere far away. In fact, I was now aware that, leaning on Mrako, I was dragging myself through the streets of Rabbat.

"What happened to me, Mrako? What time it is? Why did you do this? I trusted you! Where is Andrey?"

"Andrey? He was with us!"

"When?"

"Just moments ago, in the bar."

"Why are you lying?"

"I'm not. You just didn't recognize him."

"I would recognize my brother!"

"You know....beard, glasses, I guess that fooled you..."

"Why didn't either of you tell me?"

"Anyushka, you have to trust us. If you don't believe in our good intentions, you will be lost. You will always know what you need to know."

"I feel miserable."

He put a hand on my shoulder. For the second time. A warm breeze lifted the forelock of his black hair. A toothless drunk appeared from a side street, holding machete.

"O-ho-ho! Good evening, children! Could I please have all your money? Be quick and stay alive! C'mon, faster! I'm in a surgical mood tonight!" Mrako slowly unbuttoned his chest pocket and gave him his wallet. "Oh, that is awfully nice of you. You are good boys! Maybe too warm for my taste! Ha ha ha!" He was dirty, greasy, unshaven. He smelled of synthetic slivovitsa and garlic."

"Nice butt, Baldy!" he said, pinching my rear."

Mrako hit his neck ferociously. The stranger fell, wheezing. A bottle fell out of his jacket and booze was leaking on the sidewalk.

From another street you could hear the laughter of drunken whores.

6 WHY AM I HERE?

Every week they change our guard positions and that's how I got to spot number 3. It was easier than Nine because of better visibility. There were no woods, no hills or other obstacles that would obstruct a view of a low-flying helico. Any visit from a control officer, even theoretically, could not happen undetected. Certainly, if you were sleeping, they could surprise you. Weariness was taking a toll on me, so I had to employ some guardians' tricks. Ismail taught me how to make my time in the cold bearable. I brought my blanket and wrapped it around my torso, beneath my coat.

There was a watchtower on Three. Painted grey, it seemed to melt into the surroundings and was barely visible. With its high pillars it looked like a heron that had decided never to go south, at peace with its death and the winter, frozen.

By day I was supposed to observe from the lookout, but at night I had to patrol my area on foot. The thing was: it is hard not to climb into the watchtower and take a nap at night. This is how you do it. Over your coat you wear another coat, the one created for less severe weather conditions, then you wrap the blanket around your legs and you just sleep. That is the uncomfortable way. Ismail taught me something better. He called it the Guard's Furnace. Behind the kitchen you find a big empty can (usually from 15-kilo packs of precooked chickpeas; once a month they bring us canned food which we are supposed to distribute among ourselves). You smuggle it to the post in your backpack. You turn it upside down . Then you put a candle inside. Close to the top of the can, on the side, you make several holes with your knife. That air opening you turn toward the corner of your "cabin" so the light doesn't give you away by spreading too much. You can light your candle now. The can gets warm and generally raises the temperature a bit. It will depend on how successfully you closed all the holes and cracks around crudely- made windows and the door. Oh, yes, it is warmer now! Then you sit on an improvised chair, because you're not allowed a real chair and sitting in general is not permitted. You put your feet on the can with the candle; you cover your head with the blanket. The heat of the can will prevent your feet from freezing; the blanket will not let the warmth of your breath escape. If you take good care of your lower back, it can be very nice, a guard's paradise. The candle will quickly melt inside the can, but that was really all you needed — a 10-minute nap.

I was sleeping when the phone beeped in my pocket. I jumped in panic, not realizing where I was or what was going on. I answered the phone.

It was Mrako's voice, "You have an inspection! Captain Shaddi!" I blew out the candle and stormed down the steep stairs. The helico was already landing, scanning the ground with its lights. I reached the bushes before they were able to spot me. When its engine was cut, two people quickly emerged. They moved to the side that was draped in shadow, as looking at helico lights would quickly blind. I could still perfectly see them because I waited where they didn't expect me.

"Halt!" I cried so loudly that it echoed.

"I've stopped!" somebody replied.

"Who's there?"

"The guard corporal and the control officer."

"Corporal move forward, all others HALT!"

As the corporal started walking slowly, I lost sight of the other visitor. The steps sounded strange and I quickly repositioned on their left. That was a sight! Not only was the corporal coming towards me, but hidden behind him the control officer, too. What the hell were they playing at?

I moved behind them and screamed like a madman, "HALT or I'll shoot!"

"We've stopped!" said the corporal.

"Corporal FORWARD, all others HALT!" Emil came within whisper distance.

"Halt!"

"I have."

"Password?"

"Neon," said he.

"Nothingness," I answered. "Who is with you?" I said, my rifle still pointed at him.

" Shaddi. Captain Shaddi. You should say now, 'Others, go!'"

"Others, go forward!"

Captain Shaddi had the face of a desert rat, with oily, damaged facial skin and piercing eyes. He rattled, "Have you ever read the fucking Rules and Regulations of Guard Duty?"

"Comrade Captain, I saw it was a ruse..."

"Who the fuck do you think you're talking to?" he said very low.

He had this insane glitter in his eyes.

"Aaaatttention! Listen carefully! WHY DID YOU SAY 'halt or I will shoot'?

"You did not stop on HALT and I saw that two of

you..."

"You miserable pussy maggot! In that case you say OTHERS—HALT, and if I still don't stop you can say HALT OR I WILL SHOOT. Do you understand?"

"I do, Comrade Captain!"

"What the fuck did you just say?"

"I understand, Comrade Captain."

"You understand my dick!" He turned on his heels and rushed back to the helico. Emil just shrugged and ran after him.

I could hear Shaddi saying, "Five days for this one!"

Five days in the hole. I wasn't afraid. In a confinement, you can at least sleep at night, and sleep was the only thing you really want. I didn't have the courage to go back at the watchtower. I just walked my area and thought about the Rabbat séance. I had tried narcotics before, but had never experienced anything close to that. It felt like there was a hidden meaning to everything and it reminded me of a weird dream I had long ago... I came home from school, laid down on the couch and turned on some music. I was just listening to it, staring at a rectangle of blue sky framed by the window. I must have fallen asleep and was dreaming but what I saw in my dream was actually the same picture I was seeing while awake: a rectangle of blue sky framed by the window, only the angle from which I was looking was slightly different. Everything was dead still, like time had stopped, even though I could see clouds moving as slowly as before. The sky was gradually changing its color from light blue to purple. The time somehow stretched like this was the kingdom of slow motion. A condor was landing in the window frame. He's good, I thought. There was something royal and saintly about him. His happiness and peacefulness were irresistible. He stood in the window, looked deep in my eyes and gave me an expression that I understood as a smile.

"Who are you?" I asked.

"Your brother," replied the condor.

"My brother ?" He didn't answer. Instead, he ascended into the air. Fast. The sky was blue again.

Whatever!

For the rest of the day I felt a sweet sensation of tipsiness mingled with a strange bliss.

"Is my dream connected to the narco séance?" I asked Mrako.

He said nothing, but two days later, in a lineup for lunch, he whispered, "If you dream of a condor tonight — tell me! It's important."

After the meal we went out and smoked in front of the bunker. I wanted to hear more about the meaning of the condor, but he wouldn't say much. The time for my shift came quickly. Number 9! To punish me, Shaddi put me back on the worst sentry spot. I would probably be there for several days until all the administrative procedures were concluded. Then I would do my stint in solitary.

In a way, I liked Nine even though it could get quite uncomfortable and scary. As a space, it was the most complex. You are surrounded by woods, reeds, and marshes, and there are hills on either side. There are many ways for a potential attacker to sneak up on you. Not long before, a horrible crime was committed at Nine. The soldiers know nothing about that, it was the previous crew that got hit. Right after the incident they were dispersed all over the planet, some of them bribed by promotions or a promise of it, some by as little as a weekend off. The new crew was flown in, us. The authorities rarely release real information on what is going on. Sometimes they even keep silent about both good and bad events, but talk a lot about those that do not exist.

A special officer would often visit our post to hold a session they called a "briefing." He would basically inform us in a very complicated way about what was going on. The language they used was full of blurry phrases. Any case of a guard being killed was never openly mentioned. That would tarnish the image of the army's invincibility! Rather, it was hinted at in coded, politically correct speech. "In some guard zones, like this one, there were a few cases of undesirable incidents, the main cause of which was non-consistent execution of the Rules and Regulations of Guard Duty!"

Nine. It meant solitude, fog, and darkness. It was too far from other sentry posts so you could not possibly meet another soldier, something that we would all do, however illegal it was. If you went to a dugout, you were at risk for the helico could really surprise you by flying low over the woods or behind the hills (especially on nights with high winds when it was hard to hear it.) Potentially, the most dangerous thing for you would be if two control officers decided to do the job together. One would stay at the base to make sure the commander couldn't call the soldiers and warn them about the checkup. Another one would go on site to control and direct the pilot, thus preserving the element of surprise. That wouldn't happen very often, but it had happened in the past.

To hell with everything! I decided that a grenade never hits the same spot twice. I'd crawl into the dugout and spend my evening there. It was still day and I walked through the bushes looking for jumping porcupines. I wanted to stick my bayonet into one of them. My idea was to kill one of those animals and make myself special gloves with poisonous spikes. Those were extremely pricey in Rabbat's black market, for it was impossible to get any of these creatures in the cities. Jumpies are funny creatures. They look like a prop from children's television but if they inject their venom into you, you're done for. You'll die suffering, not from physical pain, but from unbearable mental self-torture. I spotted one, threw my knife at it, and voilà - a bull's eye! Actually, I think I was just lucky. What I didn't know and what freaked me out was that dying porcupines produce a sound that induces intense compassion in the killer. They make the saddest sounds of the killer's own species. Even in its last moments it fights to preserve itself. I stood with an improvised spear above it, confused. I had to give it up. It was crying like a baby dog.

Then, just several steps from where I stood, there was another surprise. Below the ice was the body of a dead Arijaan, woven into the long water grass, with some blood frozen to it. Somebody had been trying to melt the ice with kerosene in order to hide the corpse. Obviously, the body bobbed to the surface, got stuck on the branches that the killer had thrown in the hole to hold it down. Since temperatures were very low it froze quickly. The corpse was half-naked, skinny, with a saintly face and big open eyes that could not hide its surprise. Actually, he looked alive, only frozen. He had a desert dagger in his hand. Its crossguards were beautifully fashioned into a condor with spread wings.

When flight is silent
and wings are still,
as you ride the wind
and the desert sighs
its vast dream of grass,
remember old Aya-Hall
who used to say,
"The fish wonders
why water's wet to a Dog.
The Dog's puzzled by the condor
who circles above his master
whose stomach
contains a dead fish.
The master is confused
by the Dog's conduct.
Only the Condor is silent.
Only the Condor is free.
He lives by what-must-be."

7 WHILE THE SPIDER WEAVES HIS WEB

The black spider with three yellow dots on its back crawled towards the entangled fly. In no rush, as if doing some slow ritual dance, it was wrapping its prey in silky threads. The fly was moving less and less until it was thoroughly immobilized. Then, the spider climbed on top of the insect. The third shift came back and sentries made noise in the hall, pushing each other around the rifle racks, storing and removing their equipment. It was a fight to go to bed several minutes early. The spider had already injected his venom. The wind was whistling outside as it carried the moans and cries of generations of massacred desert dogs whose remains are to be found in stony pits all over the desert.

My third day in the hole, and finally I got some good sleep. Nobody bothered me. I don't even have to clean the bathrooms or the classroom, common treats for punished soldiers. They didn't monitor me when I had to pee or take a dump even though it was contrary to the Rules and Regulations. Mrako pretended that he was strict and treated me harshly in public. They would bring food to my cell. It was just several square meters, but big enough to let you imagine the open sky full of circling condors!

My wonderful confinement! Soldiers dream of it! Another absurdity of the military! It takes lots of guts to get put here deliberately, for you never know how exactly they might interpret your misconduct. In some complex political circumstances luck might turn its back on you and allow you to live only in the stories of your mates. There is no hard and fast rule when it comes to Rules and Regulations; that much I knew. We call them R 'n' R. Its language is extremely complicated; all kinds of legal mumbo-jumbo shaped into a kind of boring metaphor. There is a rumor that R 'n' R was created by Humans themselves. Was it?

Still, once you get in this kind of cell, it was quite refreshing. But I started torturing myself with questions. Andrey in disguise?! The condor? The corpse under the ice? The dagger's grip? When I showed it to Mrako he took it from me and hid it under his uniform. He said that it meant much more than if I had dreamed of the condor. He asked me many questions, but never sent a patrol to check the place nor did he make out a report.

Hours stretched like dough. The spider was hungry, but he wasn't in a hurry. For a long time nothing got trapped in his nets. He was approaching his meal with calmness, like a broke nobleman treated by somebody in an expensive restaurant.

It must be dark outside.

On the bed, with my eyes closed, I let my mind play movies for me. I am in the desert, in the town of Darha. In my hotel room, roller blinds and shaky ceiling fan look like a comedic attempt to protect you from the oven heat. The linens are wrinkled, and flies are buzzing. I think I hear detonations in the distance. The world is wrong. It is time that somebody pulled the carpet from under its feet and fix it. A band is playing on the street. The only words I understand in their song are sombrero and pistola. Towards the distant mountains I can see a black dot in the sky. A condor. And this is not Darha any more, it is Earthly Mexico. It is not Mexico any more. Only a room. A too small room, with no windows.

The door is opening and Mrako comes in.

"Are you OK?"

"Never been better!" He sat on my bed.

"What time of the day it is?"

"Four in the morning. Nobody's gonna come for control, not before six. The second shift left, the fire picketer is sleeping. I can take all the rifles with no problem. He wouldn't know!"

"Why did you come?" My question startled him. He was facing me, but his eyes were still not adjusted to the dark. "I wanted to see you. Is that bad?"

"The bad thing is that you never tell the truth. You're playing with me."

"What do you mean?"

"I don't mean, I know! It's obvious."

I thought I could hear the spider hooking his legs around the bumps on the wall.

"Andrey is my blood brother. His blood is mingled with mine. He saved my life once. Do you think I would play with his sister?"

"You lie, you manipulate! You are dragging me into something and you are not telling me what it is! Do you expect me to be thrilled?"

He went to the door and opened it just a crack. A beam of light fell on my bed. He took out some hush-hash from his inner pocket and started rolling a fat joint.

"It can be dangerous to reveal the truth. If you do it at the wrong time the truth can turn into a lethal lie."

"Yeah! Yadda-yadda-yadda! You're always pushing me into dreams where somehow you or somebody like you is engraving things into my psyche which will probably be used later for one of your goals. You think I'm stupid?"

"Things are not that simple."

"Just tell me the truth! Stop brainwashing me!"

He was sucking on the joint slowly. I felt that he was getting distant. The beam of light was touching his sweaty forehead.

"I won't give you a straight answer. I'll go at it slantways. Sometimes, in war, a detour is the shortest way."

It wasn't the Mrako I knew. His voice, the way he smoked and carried his body, everything about him emitted some sadness. He looked weak and vulnerable.

"It's quite possible that I was born in Darha."

That surprised me. Why was he telling me this when the Committee's recommendation was not to talk about one's personal past? He kept talking, staring at the wall as though he was able to see through it, looking at the deserts of his childhood.

"Maybe I wasn't born there, but they certainly found me there, in an old Python. I was a premature baby and everybody wondered how I survived. They sent me to the Bureau for Genetic Research where they played with me for several months, only to pass me on later to the state orphanage. From there, I was given up for adoption. I ended up in the family of an old street musician and shoe polisher called Vlastimir. My adopted mother, Zvezdana, got killed and the whole world went upside down. I still remember her smile, her scent, the way she would caress my hair. She still comes in my dreams to take care of me or to give me advice. There, she would cook for me and I would wake up without feeling hungry. My mother was the most beautiful creature in the world. Dad had lots of health troubles and he wasn't able to bring enough bread home. It was something to do with his brain. My parents were great people who will live in my heart as long as it beats. Their marriage was good and very stable; I don't remember them ever fighting. They couldn't have kids, but they had me and

I received all the love a child could have. Some would think that what united them so strongly was the fact that they lived at the very bottom of society and to fall lower was impossible. That's not true. It was the love they somehow had for each other and that spread to me. There was no poorer shack than ours in Darha's lumpen ring. What money they had went towards feeding me, but they ate from the garbage of the proletariat. I can never forget that. Mom had a dream that the old man would get permission to sift through Human garbage. Some distant cousin, who in their eyes was an influential bureaucrat, was supposed to help us get a permit, but he constantly asked for new presents for his superiors, milking from my parents whatever they still had. Sure, it turned out he just lied and took everything for himself. Those were not good years for dogs in Darha. Several bombs exploded in shopping malls, then at a train station and on the city train. After those incidents that were supposedly organized by some ultra-left group called DAO came the sanctions ...You probably heard of it. I can tell you — it was all lies. No Arijaan ever had any knowledge of any such group...Anyways, the result would always be the same, new sanctions against Darha's dogs. And who do you think they hit the hardest? Us — the poorest of poor dogs! Where were you then? In a daycare? On vacation? At some fancy seaside resort? And me? I was just learning how to steal and how to avoid drunks that rape little boys. I had an old metal barrel. Sometimes, I would go there in the afternoon and simply enjoyed being alone with my imagination. My barrel would become a spaceship. It was hidden in bushes and I was hidden in it. I had a view of an abandoned park, given up by the authorities long ago. Couples would come there to make love and that was my big chance. While they were busy with themselves I would sneak and go through their clothes. I'd steal anything I could find. I remember that once it was a corkscrew. Well, that place marked me for life. I'll tell you how.

One late afternoon a black Cortina drove into my woods. It was as shiny as a general's boots. I expected a good haul. I could see a Human inside, disgustingly colorless, soft and smooth.

And who was with him? My mother. My blood was boiling. This Human was dangling a money bill over her head while she was doing something to him. I grab a big stone and throw it at the car. The windshield cracks. The Human takes his gun and aims it at me. My mother bites him. He grabs her hair and, half naked, drags her out of the car. I kicked the bastard, but I couldn't hurt him. He wants to shoot at me. Mom pushes him. He missed me. He was about to fire a second shot when she started screaming. He shoots her. I start running away. He shoots her in the head and the noise stops. I stop, too, paralyzed. I'm not interesting to him anymore. He looks at me as if I were a potato dug from an unexpected place. He shrugs and leaves.

I couldn't talk for months. They put me in a hospital for the mentally ill, but then I said something and that was enough for them to announce that I was healthy and to kick me out. Back home, it wasn't good. Dad was sick. Something with his brain kept complicating. He still taught me how to talk to the authorities and to make an application for military school. I passed all the tests and was accepted. Nobody there cared about my past, or class. For the army, your life starts in the army and is judged only based on how you do your military assignments. Those orphan dogs have no past. The day the state takes them under its wing is the day of their birth. Strangely, that was first time I felt equal to others. For example, your brother was treated the same as I was even though he came from the highest class of dogs. Soon, my dad died.

I thought I was alone in the world, but I had shelter and food and even some friends. In Grade Seven we were at boot camp in the desert Rag-O. We were taught to find and destroy underground villages. Following the instructions of the theoretical part of the training I actually found an entrance into a system of underground passages. Actually, it was not exactly the entrance, more something like a big masked vent, hidden between red rocks. Skinny as I was, I easily crept in and came to some big opening, more like a huge room, the size of an average high school gym. Several tunnels began there. It looked like an abandoned mine except that the walls were covered with drawings and writings. The alphabet I didn't know, it looked a bit like a variation of the alphabet from the movie The Possessed. I went on further without thinking much. When I came to another crossroad the whole thing repeated. I just knew which way to take and I took it."

Mrako paused. He swallowed his saliva. He was far away, in those mysterious halls and tunnels. The spider was hanging on the silky thread, swaying like a bored kid on a swing.

"Then, some whisper registered, echoed within me, calling my name. I got scared and grabbed my gun. There was some shaky light around the corner. I turned my flashlight off but the whispering didn't stop. The huge cave was before me with all those luxurious natural decorations we could see at school. In the middle, the stalactites and stalagmites were trimmed, giving an illusion of a room or a podium. There were many lit candles there, those archaic ones, made from beeswax. Their light and shadows made the whole place look exceptionally complex. Flames were waving in a breeze and the room was constantly reshaping itself because of it. In the middle, on an old rag, sat a monk with long grey hair and beard. He wore simple peasant's clothes full of holes. His head was positioned like he was trying to see where the end of an ocean is. That dog looked like he was not part of this world. In fact, I thought that he did not notice my presence. He stretched his hands and with slow rotating movements gently rubbed the surface of something that I couldn't see. The "caressing zone" slowly turned into a cube of pink light. A violent, sudden wind emerged from it and veered straight to me. I thought it was taking the flesh off my bones. I cried and begged, but the wind became its opposite. Now, it was like I was being sucked in by a giant vacuum cleaner. I was flying over the desert with another condor. And I saw: a snake that slithers between rocks, a hunter who was setting his traps, armed dogs protecting Humans, Humans testing new hybrids of agricultural dogs, dogs shining shoes for other dogs, the ghost of my mother aimlessly walking the roads, Arijaan villages being swallowed by fire, bombed by the army I serve, a pine tree that was extracting its own sap, a Human cutting a tree, making a fire, and roasting meat."

There is a weeping story in every being, I thought, but didn't say anything.

"I blinked," said Mrako. I said nothing. He talked like he didn't expect anybody to interrupt.

"I blinked, and I was back in the cave, sitting in front of the old monk, my legs crossed, spine stiff and straight. He pulled out a dagger and lifted it slowly to the middle of the imaginary line that connected my irises to his. He opened his fingers and let the dagger levitate. Its crossguard was shaped like a condor with wings spread. I felt I was in a dream, where you usually do things without thinking. I kissed the dagger."

A loud noise suddenly emerged from the hall. The Corporal was waking up the third shift. Mrako ran out, locking the door of my sweet prison.

Silence.

I couldn't see the spider any more. I knew he was waiting somewhere with the patience that only spiders have.

8 ISMAIL'S HEAD

They put me back on Nine. I had gotten so used to my prison that the idea of returning to watch duty was hard to take. Guards say that shifts last forever while the weeks fly. At our base everybody seemed to be down. It was interesting how little things like water restrictions can change your mood. If you were unlucky the water would come while you are on your shift and who knew when the next opportunity to have a shower or even wash your hands would come. Lots of it had to do with our apathy; we were all too lazy to do anything. The bathroom hadn't been cleaned, which meant that there was a pyramid of shit in every stall. It gave a certain aroma to the whole building. In the morning, when a control officer might come, everything looked fine, but during the day those pyramids restored themselves. Nobody cared. At some point, every guard crew in the world hit this stage of indifference. It was a result of a constant lack of sleep.

All of this meant that our protection of the zone was not in good shape. Nobody cared about that either. Mrako enforced cleaning only in the mornings. Corporals Emil and Midagar appeared to be either absent-minded or relaxed. I wasn't any different. I had no fear of the authorities or anybody else. Life and death were similar; in fact they were the same: topics I don't want to think about. But then something happened.

The new helico pilot enjoyed shaking soldiers' kidneys with his rough landings. At the end of the shift, I wanted to smash his face. Emil was already announcing our arrival at Nine and I had to jump out. The old guard was not there. Emil told me to quickly scan the area. The helico could wait. Everybody thought that the stubborn highlander was sleeping somewhere and guys started making fun of him. All of us had learned a bunch of crafty sleeping tricks from Ismail. Now, he'd be caught sleeping. Not much would come of it since there was no control officer with us, but I knew he'd be mocked for weeks.

He was not at the watchtower or in the bushes. For sure, he went to the dugout! Where else could he be? Carefully, not to be seen by the others, I went into the bush that covered the entrance. I called his name, and scanned around with a flashlight. It was empty. Outside, Emil was already yelling, rushing me to find "the bastard."

"I can't find him!" I yelled back, but they couldn't hear me because of the helico's noise. I made signs with my hands and Emil and all the soldiers emerged and we started combing the area. The mood changed, and everybody became quiet. A cold wind whistled through the trees and the bushes, chilling our bones. Then we heard a scream. It was nothing: a soldier startled by a jumping porcupine. Several minutes after, Ismail was found. He was in sitting position, leaning on an old tree, supporting with his right hand his own severed head in the same way ancient knights carried their helmets. His eyes were open, and calm. There was no expression of surprise on his face, just as though he was watching a show neither interesting nor boring. His winter jacket was open and a big stain of frozen blood at the level of his heart.

Noise and swearing. Packing the corpse...They left. I stayed.

Alone.

Over the phone Mrako told me to call if I noticed anything unusual. That was it.

Silence.

Silence was raveling my nerves like an old knitted sweater. A sweater was actually being untied and transformed into a wool ball. This wool ball was heavy. I cried in the bushes, saying to myself, why do I have to go through all of this? I am just a girl!

When the helico finally came I was so happy to see it. At the base, everybody was quiet. Mrako was typing his report. We lay on our beds, but nobody slept. A fecal stench nested in every throat. The fire picketer smoked in the hall. Midagar walked up and down with his headphones. Three hours passed quickly. I didn't sleep, but I had to go back to my shift. Nobody was slowing down preparations, or trying to buy time indoors. We were early, with our fear advising, "Run! Run to your destiny!"

Nine was next. I felt tension in my stomach and tried to hide it. As soon as the helico was gone I went into the dugout and lit the lamp. Inside: a couple of rugs, empty cans full of melted candle wax, a porn magazine. Nonetheless, it was much warmer here. I wrapped myself in rugs, secured the entrance with pieces of wood, tied a rope to it and another to my pinky, unlocked my rifle, cocked it and fell asleep.

Immediately: a dream. I am in the Rag-O desert. I am standing, but my legs ache. I sit and suddenly it's night. I hear thunder in the distance, but it's not getting closer nor it is going away, rather it's circling. I looked towards the stars and I saw the shadow of a condor. Drawing a spiral, he was coming towards me.

It landed.

"Hello!" I say.

"It is time for you to learn how to fly," he said in a stern voice. I just shrugged. "After you drink the blue of the sky, you come to the ground only to sleep or eat."

"I am just a dog. A bitch! Why should I fly?"

"We are all dogs and bitches, spiders and birds and salamanders! The essence is about living uninhibited."

"How can I live uninhibited?"

"Let the truth dismember you. Then, start learning. On the path to a Great Battle every destiny will be good."

Everything sank into darkness and from there a giant glowing fly appeared, making the same type of noise a helico would. As it got closer it became obvious that it was Ismail's severed head. His face had a mild, gentle expression.

"They lied to us, my friend. We know nothing about the world, about battle, about ourselves. We think that serving is natural, that dogs are destined to gnaw the bones. Look in my eyes. Look!"

In his blue, saintly eyes I saw a soldier slitting the throat of an Arijaan child, a journalist writing a fake report from a battlefield, secret meetings where strange dogs discuss Freedom, my parents when they were young, walking along the river in which I was hopelessly sinking.

It wasn't Ismail's head. It was Andrey!

"You, Andrey!?"

"It's me."

"Andrey, I'm going crazy! Why do you play with me?"

"Nobody's playing with you. Some things must happen. That is what our struggle demands of us. You know nothing about this system. You think that our father is a lovely man who does everything in his life according to honor. We just tried to open your eyes and make you hatch. To bring you to the Truth. And this is your response? 'Why do you play with me?' Can't you understand? Can you not see? It's a war! A big one, a holy one, a war for liberation of our species, of dogkind! Yes, we were artificially created, designed to be lower beings, a cheap labor force. But I say WE HAVE THE RIGHT TO WATER AND WIND, SADNESS AND LAUGHTER, TO THOUGHTS AND DREAMS! WE ARE A SPECIES! WE ARE ALIVE! We have consciousness, we thirst for freedom! War is the only way to achieve this! They will never let us be free. Freedom is something you must earn through fighting. The enemy is much stronger, but the history of this universe is a story about fights against superior powers. We are not a hybrid, remember it! We are a species! We want independence! We just want to peacefully live in our deserts. The Organization will win this battle! It is always like that, Anya! The future comes from the bottom while those on top sink in the past. Is there on this shitty planet any other bottom but us? You know nothing, Anyushka! You were raised in a golden cage and its comfort has blinded you. It is not only eyes that see! Millions of dogs see with their stomachs and that picture is blurred by hunger! It is their turn to write on the blank pages of history!"

He paused, as if in a dilemma.

"We are programmed to obey, to be down. I say the program must be destroyed! Maybe Mrako told you... there are old dogs in the deserts who guard the knowledge of dreaming, our beautiful secret, the teaching that will elevate us to Freedom. As you know, the founder was Aya-Hall, the desert shaman, the shaman of all shamans. He said, 'Consciousness has to be smashed, for only from its ruins will free being arise.' We are, dear Anyushka, successors of that teaching, but something more, too. We are Revolution, we walk through the fire. The fire we carry in us is looking for a vent now. For centuries, narcotics were the only way to feel uninhibited. We cherish our tradition, but we're upgrading it: we aim our dreams. Mrako, I, and many other comrades went through training to achieve this. Revolution is our only path. According to Aya-Hall, a Condor is an incarnation of it. Poetic master of altitudes that kills ground-walking creatures and eats corpses! He's a big cleaner. Look, Anyushka, we're birds!"

Indeed, we flew. And deserts were as vast as oceans and oceans were as vast as deserts. Cities — rings that fitted into each other. A luxurious Human Core in the middle, then the ring of rich dogs, the middle class, the poor, and the super-poor lumpens (dog-dogs). The ring of forbidden valleys, the ring of minefields, the guard zone and then the desert. If the Arijaans ever attacked a city they would have to kill lots of city-dogs before they even got close to Humans. For city-dogs the Arijaans are barbarians who will rape their wives and kill their children.

Andrey started nose-diving. We descended fast, our beaks aimed at the ground. At the moment when we were supposed to hit the floor and break our necks I woke up!

Darkness. All around me darkness.

My feet are cold.

Watery slime is dripping from my nose.

The candle is snuffed off. I look at my watch. The shift will end soon. I go out to wait for the change of shift, bouncing to heat myself up. Jumping porcupines are moaning far away. Nobody is around. I light a cigarette, hiding it inside my palm. The air that I breathe out hardly makes it before it drops on my chest like a frost. So many stars are in the sky. One of them is the Sun. Tonight, you can barely see its blinking, but you could hear the helico engines in the distance.

VISION

Rolling back my eyes,
Under the moldy dome,
In a haze of lies
I see my Rome.

The birds in the sky

Just drew the fate
And all we can do
Is to be late.

The gold will melt,
The bread will bleed
And those who knelt
Will crush the greed.

With this inner sight
I fight in vain,
Like a tree before a lumberjack,
I remain.

9 AT HOME

Everything around me seemed so familiar and so strange. Carpets on the floors! Lace curtains! Ceramic tiles in the bathroom! I could cry. It felt like a thousand years had passed since I left. Those expensive things didn't exist in my mind anymore. Busovaccha tea-cups! Unreal! Andrey was sitting in the chair across the room from our father. Mother cried at first, but she was glowing now, her son and her daughter were back! Yet there was a tension in the room. All the servants were sent to the kitchen.

Andrey: I am responsible for her! She is on the right path.

Father: And what would that "right path" be?

Andrey: I can't talk about that.

Father: I was so proud of you! My son was going to be an officer of The Guard! And now!? What should I think? You take your sister somewhere and you don't even ask or explain!

Andrey: I would if I could.

Father: You are hiding something, something that's not good for any of us. I can see that.

Andrey: This system is rotten! As a wet rotten cloth that

spreads its festering stink!

Father: You are young and you don't know much.

Andrey: When I was five I didn't decide what I'd be in life.

Father: Son, everything I ever did was for the good of my children. God is my witness. Your mother knows. She's the same. Don't do anything that'll bring shame on the family name. We were always honorable dogs that worked for the system's improvement.

Andrey: Cry, mother, cry! Everybody lives according to his or her own conscience. Everybody has a choice. You can fulfill your destiny, chase your dreams, you can hunt what can't be caught. I am talking about FREEDOM. You don't understand me. The very concept is alien to you. You think that there's Freedom in serving?

I couldn't listen to this anymore. I went to my room and turned on the radio. The latest hit was on.

I drank every night
in Zee-Zee Pub
wanting to forget you.
but every morning,
on the streets,
Your scent waited for me.

I knew mother was shocked by my appearance. She was always like that. After being away for such a short time, my home was alien to me! It felt like a sweet memory of something that didn't exist anymore. It was like an old song you were fond of long ago, but it sounded obsolete now. I go back to the living room.

Andrey: We are strangers, father. I barely remember you. You were for me just like a sweet fiction. So, what do you want me to choose? Fiction or a battle I believe in?

Father: One can lose his head talking like that! You have to know that everything we enjoy on this planet is achieved with lots of sacrifice and hardship. We descend from those who were expelled from their home planet, expelled to a new place that was so unfriendly and looked like hell. The chances of survival were really small. Those exiles were both Humans and dogs, they had to pay a high price for the progressive ideas they held. And what did they do here? They made a new civilization, a brotherly unity of Humans and dogs!

Andrey: Where a brother backstabs his brother! One brother lives in poverty and another one, who is rich, talks about progress and peace?

Mother was watering her plants, her hands shook and water was falling on the carpet.

Father: That is the way things have to be. Humans are more intelligent, and stronger. They are wiser than us. They have no other choice but to provide leadership.

Andrey: You really believe that?!

Father: I do. If I didn't, my life would make no sense!

Andrey: Your life makes no sense anyway. It looks you were created to lick the bone clean and to be happy about it. Well, you grabbed one of the biggest ones!

Father: Nobody ever insulted me that much. Please, leave now.

Andrey: We are warriors, father! This is not the time for tears. Don't surrender to emotions so easily. That is the method the Humans have chosen for us to serve them: to lie on our backs and wag our tails! We have to look within and rediscover our lupine heritage.

Mother stood still by the window. She was crying with no sound. Father was looking at the floor.

"Please, just go." said he.

I followed Andrey. What remained behind was an ugly gap. We walked the streets of Chortwille, but I paid no heed to anything. I saw nothing except my brother's head, his strong and decisive steps that led us back to Rabbat.

Music. Belly dancers. Some mysterious stranger who

talked with Andrey in whispers. And Andrey who said, "The different world will come, the different world. We will die singing, for our death and our lives will have meaning. The different world will come, the different world! This rot and pus will be gone! The wind and the rain will carry the dirt away. Dust to dust! Cheers!"

We went upstairs with the stranger. The hotel looked like a cheap whorehouse. The room had no windows. Walls, floor and ceiling were all black. I felt some fear. Death is the only thing I could think of. It was dark as a tomb. Sadness took me as big clouds swallowed mountains. I couldn't forget the pain in my father's eyes. They closed the door. We sat on the floor. Andrey whispered like a psychotic priest from morning TV.

"There is snow all around us. Eternal winter and eternal ice! Any dog can live in a desert, but in every heart there will be pain until every brother is free. Those who do not want Freedom have already chosen Death! Tell us, our brother, why did destiny make us meet?"

The stranger replied, "You will soon be in the Naked Cave. You don't have to ask about it. It will just happen. The storm that's coming will be divine. This room is a simple example of the space where you will charge your batteries for the big deeds you are honored to do. This is our weapon! The dreams will help us recognize our ways when we are awake. To live free, uninhibited! Do you hear the waves of the ocean? Don't you feel the scent of the breeze? Revolution will need us to be birds and wolves. And wolves will emerge!"

Understanding nothing,
I raise my cross high.
Following the hammer's rhythm,
Through flaming cities
And ghostly inns
I sail to the mainland!

10 BRIEFING

There was no sleep for the soldiers that night.

Mrako said, "Nobody can even think of sitting down until everything shines like a new car!"

Brooms, clothes, detergent, chlorine! No stopping. Before dawn, everything was finally done so we hoped that those who don't have to go for a shift would be allowed to sleep. However, he commanded that everybody go into the classroom "shaved and clean, looking like a real soldier." They even put a flag of our world on the wall, half black and half red, with circles of opposite colors in the middle of each field. Everything in this world has two shadows, every kid knows that, but not everybody understands. Two shadows!

We sat and complained quietly.

Once in a while, Mrako would hit the table with his palm. He swore, calling us faggots and threatening us with punishments. For the first time, I felt capable of hating him. Suddenly, the door opened and Captain Shaddi pompously marched into the room.

"A-tten-tion!" shouted Mrako.

We all jumped at the same time. The desert rat, Captain

Shaddi, had the expression of someone who is constipated and suffers from hemorrhoids. I should have liked him, he was the one who gave me confinement, but it was hard to feel sympathetic towards that ugly face.

"Comrades! Soldiers! Guardians!" he said. "Most of you already know me, but I will introduce myself again. I am Captain Shaddi, security officer for this region. Why am I here today? You know that we are practically at war even though it has not been officially declared. We can't be sure that the Arijaan offensive against our city will not start this very day. I don't want to bother you with warnings about how alert you must be nor do I have to remind you how lucky we should feel for we live on this planet of freedom and dignity. We are on a degree of high alert. I don't need to repeat how everything must be done in accordance with the Rules and Regulations. In this situation, the highest law is chapter 12. It means: make a mistake, and you'll be executed. Now, I want to start our informational session. One of your comrades was murdered. In another city the whole guard squad was killed. Our security is in question! It's not only dangerous at your guard post, but also in your base, in the dorm, the kitchen, anywhere. In one town two shifts were killed together with the commander, corporals and driver. These are just examples."

His head, moving at an even speed, panned the room.

"At the beginning, the enemy was trying to create a rift in the brotherhood between Humans and dogs, but once they realized that task was impossible they started a series of cowardly terrorist attacks. Comrades, Guardians, you have to be alert in every moment. They are organized in groups of three, so-called Triangles. Their goal is to infiltrate themselves, to become part of us and try to spread the cancer of their illusions amongst us. Even more than that, they want to control the situation in every zone so when the moment comes they march into our cities with as little trouble as possible. The very idea is suicidal. If they ever try, they will be badly defeated. However, I don't think they share my opinion. The situation is serious."

This master of dramatic pauses inhaled deeply, then sighed.

"We don't want to lose a single soldier or citizen! I am telling you: we will fight with the conviction that only justice can give us. The brotherhood will not be broken! It is the foundation of the world we built. This freedom did not come easy. Together with Humans, we fought for it. We will not let anybody spit on the results of that struggle. Both the Arijaans and we are dogs, but the difference between us and them is much bigger than the difference between us and Humans. The Arijaans descended from criminals, foes of progress and sexual maniacs, lazy punks that never wanted to do honest work, but preferred to live as parasites. As we were building our free world they were forced to retreat to the deserts the same way rats avoid clean places and daylight. In other words, they were escaping legal punishments for the crimes they had committed in the cities. From garbage ancestors garbage people arose! We must weed out our fields of liberty and show no mercy. That is the task our history has placed before us."

I had the feeling that I heard somewhere this style of oratory. Maybe in some movie. He must have watched it a million times. Shaddi was looking up through the ceiling.

"Why did I talk about this?" His eyes were cutting the air. He pointed his finger at me.

"You, soldier!"

"Yes, Comrade Captain!"

"Why am I talking about this?"

"You want us to be aware that the Arijaan attack might happen at any time."

"You knew that before!" He laughed ironically.

"But we didn't know that we had to be careful even in our bedroom! That any comrade might be a traitor waiting to slit your throat! That means that from now on our guard duty never stops. We can't trust anybody any more. We must examine everything. Anybody could be working for the enemy or be the enemy. I think that's what you wanted to say."

"Very good, soldier! Very good!"

"I understand, Comrade Captain! I serve my people!"

Shaddi walked the classroom in silence. Corporal Emil and two other soldiers were sleeping.

"Aaaaaa-ttention!" screamed Shaddi.

Everybody jumped, except those three. The captain gave us the sign to be quiet. He approached Emil and yelled in his ear, "Aaaaaaa-tention!"

All three woke up. Emil looked lost, but he realized what had just happened.

"You, corporal!"

"Yes, Comrade Captain! Lance corporal Emil Borucinsky at your service!"

"You are sleeping!!!"

"It was not my intention, Comrade Captain! I am very tired."

"You two! Come here!" said Comrade Captain.

Frightened, Taffa and Zeka approached. Shaddi, obviously inspired, barked the following rhymes,

"Commander, these two slobs
Should get the worst possible jobs.
I'd give them a month in confinement,
But I am the man of refinement!
To be a soldier, not a piece of junk,
This corporal will lose his rank."

Then he turned to the audience.

"Let our sleeping beauty
Do regular guard duty!
To end this stanza of mine,
Give him number Nine!"

Everybody laughed. Shaddi was enjoying his rhyming skills.

"And, yes, I almost forgot — this soldier deserves a shot! He does not sleep and he knows answers! Well, hand him the corporal's duties! Confirmation of his rank will come from the command post in a couple of days. You understand?"

"I understand, Comrade Captain!" said Mrako.

As Shaddi was heading towards the exit one of the soldiers shouted, "But he was recently in confinement!"

"I know how you feel
But luck is a spinning wheel!"
replied Shaddi.

We sit in Mrako's office. Emil is sipping vodka. Mrako asks him if he feels indifferent and Emil just shrugs and says that he feels sleepy. The office is painted black, its windows covered. Now, it's an "energy collector"

"We are a Triangle, ain't we?" I ask Mrako.

"Triangle... he he... it really doesn't matter. We just invented that hoax as a way to joke with them. There is a whole theory of our sacred system of numbers that our guys invented just to give the enemy a hope that they can understand us and predict our actions. Total crap!"

"Is it?"

"Well, maybe not completely. We always do things according to the number 3. There is a special team designing that whole theorem, so to speak, something that you can eventually decode. We play with them as they play with us. One day they'll think that they know our next move and then we'll do something else, unexpected and out of the pattern. Yet I would not waste any energy thinking about it. Knowing the Committee, they might surprise us, too. What do you think? Is it three or four of us?"

Midagar just brought his shift. He was putting ammo cartridges back in the safe, occasionally checking them out.

Mrako told him what had just happened and that I was a newly promoted corporal. Midagar's pupils shrank.

"Good for you!" he said, putting an accent on "you."

"Corporal Andrey! It might sound goofy! Not because he can't do the job, but he is still a lizard, he has a lot to learn. Will the jombas get up from their beds when he tries to wake them?" Jombas were old soldiers.

"We'll see," I said.

He just looked at me with a mixture of boredom and contempt and, grabbing three daily snack rations even though he's only entitled to one, walked out of the office.

"When he's around, be careful. Don't talk too much," Mrako said.

"Why? Is he the zinc-master?"

"I think so... the biggest in Ratville."

"He works for Shaddi," Emil added.

"Why did you never tell me that? Emil is one of us?"

"Instead of Mrako, "Emil replied. "And why would we tell you? You could feel it. The condor can feel anything."

Laughing, he left the room.

"Condor, condor, condor! I'm not getting it! Why it is so important to all of you?" I asked Mrako.

"Humans have uncomfortable thoughts regarding the bird. It reminds them of death and they are afraid to think about death. Animals don't have such fears, while for man it's a constant reminder that they are not immortal and that they will, in one way or another, be eaten in the end. The Condor could spread his wings wider than any known bird; he was the master of the sky. There is nobody who could endanger him. I don't know how much you've read, but for us that bird is a symbol of freedom, freedom from predators, but also from fears. Unlike the Human concept, our idea of Liberty includes the idea of being at peace with your own death. That is why we are not afraid to die, that's why we like to think we are already dead. We appreciate life more. There's a purpose to it."

"How did you influence my mind so that I had that dream with the condor in it, and even became one?"

"I focused my mental energy on you. I was ordered to do that. Andrey was insisting that you join the cause and my assignment was to initiate your dusha, your soul, your soft side, your sadness for the world."

"What do you mean?"

"It doesn't have to be important for you now. The technique is ancient; nobody remembers when it was crafted. It might have been inherited from Earthly proto-dogs. What is certain is that it's part of the religious teachings of Aya-Hall. His followers, Hallases, are priests. In natural or artificial underground caves, they dream of freedom. They pursue visions of the exalted state of living unrestricted. Well, that provided for the spiritual and cultural survival of Arijaans through our dark centuries of slavery. If you can't dream of something you will never get it... and even if you do get it by some kind of weird accident — you won't know what to do with it. Aya-Hall was teaching: 'If you nurture your soul long enough with certain visions, they will stop being images and will turn into the world itself.' That, my dear, means: Your soul, your dusha, will either start seeing the world as it does in your visions or it will push you to constantly change reality so that you can bring it closer to the ideal you see. The first way would be the way of priests. The second one is the path of warriors, dogs like Andrey or me. Or you... We respect the teaching of Aya-Hall, but our path is not just dreaming, it is also doing! Revolution! Revolution is our way! It doesn't mean that we reject the Hallas philosophy! That's what made us. Without it we would be just a bunch of bloodthirsty thugs!"

"Is Andrey sane?"

"That's a ridiculous question! How can you ask something like that?"

"I don't know... when he talked with our father everything was... hard to say... I knew I couldn't stay at home, something was pulling me here, but I felt some coldness in Andrey... a terrifying ice... You know, his words are all fire, but his heart is cold. I cannot believe that he is a Hallas, too."

"He is. He's a Hallas-Nail, the one who goes through! Merciless and sharp! His spirit, his body, all of him — a Nail! And visions? Visions are more like the hammer, the striking power."

For a moment, something broke in me. I could see my parents silently sitting in the living room, staring at the door. A tear slid down my cheek. Mrako said nothing, yet he remained seated next to me. He hugged me.

I will buy yellow pants,
Yellow pants I will buy,
So, when you walk home
You can see me, leaning on the fence,
Mysterious and alone.
Oh, yellow pants, yellow pants,
Oh, yellow pants I will buy!

11 NIGHTMARES OF THE ZONE

My first shift as a corporal, and there was an accident! We landed on Five, but a guardian, a fellow called Victor Troha, was not waiting for a helico. He was far from the spot, rolling on the ground, running, jumping, and screaming. He looked funny in a way. By the gleam in his bloody eyes we knew what it was: a jumping porcupine. It didn't matter anymore how it happened. In about 20 hours he'd be gone. We tied him to the helico's cage and continued on with the exchange route. There was no hope for him.

I could see in the mirror the jerking spasms of his face, his mouth opening, and some of his mates laughing at him. I called the base to tell them about the accident so they wouldn't be surprised when we come. In cases like this there was no use in calling an ambulance, the Rule leaves to the commander to decide what should be done with the unlucky fellow. Mrako told us not to kill him, which I wouldn't do anyway. There is always some hope or, at least, one wants to think so. Tied up salami style, we laid him on the bed in the confinement room and locked the door. May his agony be short!

"God is my witness! It was not my responsibility! Crepes with apricot jam!" he screamed like he was giving a speech at a packed stadium.

"Nobody has the right to blame me for that! I wasn't informed. When I came they were on the table and I just thought they were left for me. I had no idea that Milanka hadn't even tried them! My Lord, I ate them all! I gobbled them all!" He screamed and cried, he cried and screamed and looked like his dusha was being torn apart.

"Why are you standing there?" said Mrako in his commander's voice.

"I've never heard something like this."

"The first thing to do when you get back is to put all the ammunition in the safe."

"Safe! It's a shelf with a cheap metal door on it."

"Shelf or not, it's metal. That's what we have, all the ammo has to be locked! While you are putting cartridges in the SAFE, you must check the hole on each of them so you at least know if there are 30 bullets in there. If it's black, a bullet is missing. You report it to me immediately and whose cartridge it was. You saw Emil doing it. Just do the same. If you think anything is suspicious, you take all the bullets out and count them. A soldier can put an empty shell in the middle so everything looks fine. Every lost bullet means that one of us could be killed. If a certain guard looks suspicious to you, always count his bullets. Sometimes you do it for all the cartridges, sometimes you choose randomly. This is important. If you fail to spot a steal and you are caught you're in deep shit. No God can help you in Military Court."

"I understand. But aren't we all possible suspects, even you and me?"

"Shut the fuck up!" he whispered. "You never know who is... And don't listen to this poor soul... You're not able to help him, yet he's able to screw you up. Remember that." I nodded and checked the cartridges, counted the ammo, especially Victor's. He could have shot the bloody porcupine, but it was all there. The animal and he met unexpectedly and the porcupine was faster.

"You didn't decide to have Victor killed?" I asked Mrako.

"No. I thought there might be some chance."

"You weren't that sentimental when Ismail got murdered. His death didn't touch you as much."

"That was different."

"Different? How?"

"Anya, since I met you, you are always provoking me, accusing me of something."

"Would you tell me how could I not? Don't you see that it's about lives?"

"Anya, Ismail had it coming. He deserved it."

"Nobody deserves to end up sitting with his chopped-off head placed in his own lap!"

"Correct, but I can also tell you that nobody deserves to end up not even buried, with no name, under the ice. Ismail murdered that Arijaan, robbed him and murdered him in cold blood. He caught him while he was trying to pass through the Zone to enter the city. Arijaan admitted everything, he was going to Chortwille, to a rich dog's ring where he intended to find and kill some doberman lieutenant who beheaded his wife and daughter. Ismail instructed him to go back and return in two days, at the time of his shift. Arijaan was supposed to bring half a kilo of gold and a kilo of desert heroin. In exchange, Ismail would let him go through the Zone and provide him with the doberman's whereabouts. The poor guy believed him and when Ismail finally got the desired goods he just got rid of the sucker. The knife you found in his palm says that the Arijaan was once a Hallas, a Hallas who under the weight of his sorrow lost his discipline and judgment and became an ordinary foolish dog."

How in the hell does he know this, I thought, but said

nothing, just kept sorting Victor's cartridges and locked the safe. Midagar entered the room.

"How are things, officer?" he goaded.

"Not too good. Victor got porcupined."

"Ha ha ha! I heard! He's shitting all the time about some crepes and about school. And he's whining about some test he didn't do well, an Understanding of Nature and Society test in which he claims he was best in the class. Funny way to die, eh?"

"Your sense of humor is disgusting!" said Mrako.

"What do you want me to do? Be a crybaby? No, dude, I'm not taking that path! I wonder what's for dinner."

"Bean soup, what else would it be."

"Or macaroni!" I added.

"Yup. From this shitty food we are all getting bellies. They fill us with starch! We all have these funny female stomachs... It's like we all have a period!"

Again, we could hear Victor scream, "She was like a doe, her skin pale and soft and when she smiled some sadness gleamed in her eyes. She was like our suns, when they are setting and the world seems to disintegrate in their vanishing light. She would always order a coffee, and smile. I felt that there was a special meaning to that smile, but I couldn't figure it out. I had a huge urge to protect her, but every day I was getting lost even more."

Midagar went to the hall so he could hear better. He was laughing his ass off.

"Once I wanted to give her a gift, something very special, but, dear lord, how can any present be special enough to match her eyes, that beautiful sadness that falls on the world like morning mist, that sugary fog that rolls over hills like a hundred cellos playing some low, melancholic drone. I decided to make something, something that can't be utilized. I took a box of fireplace matches; there was a picture of an old-fashioned key on it. I put a dried rosebud inside. I wanted it to be a poem written with tiny objects, a love poem that you can read in many ways and never lose its main message. So I put some things inside. For example, one of them was tiny tube of paper and when you unfold it you could see mysterious signs whose meaning I didn't know but that looked as sweet and as disturbing as love itself. I just invented them, or at least I invented their combination: an old Egyptian bird sign; an upside-down cross; an open eye; two arrows, parallel but pointed in opposite directions; and who knows what else. I wrote with my blood, blood from my ring finger. I inserted two plastic heads, one male and one female, not bigger than cherry pits, five plastic orange pearls on a string, a tiny perfume bottle filled with pieces of cinnamon, hashish, and some of my nail-clippings and hair.

We walked along the river. Water whispered on our left side and on our right was an orchard. I suddenly remembered a true story I had heard long ago, and started telling it.

There was a young woman, a teacher, who was sent to work in the countryside. One summer she met a student of philosophy and started liking him very much. Every word he said she'd take as a thirsty mouth swallows water, as nature accepts the sunshine in the spring, with submissive gratitude. And her student, well, he could talk. Mostly about history, and society and how materialistic philosophy doesn't buy into any mythological or religious crap and she just listened, her dusha enthralled. The summer was unfolding and they were in love. Soon, they started planning their wedding and everything looked wonderful. I forgot to mention that several nights before she had a very weird dream. She was going through the field and along the river bank and there were no trees anywhere except one big cherry tree, almost as big as an oak. It was hot in that dream so she naturally started walking towards the tree's shade and when she arrived a big surprise awaited her. Under the branches bent down from the weight of their fruit, on a rattan chair, in a white suit, sat her dead father. She wanted to say something, but only cried and smiled and her father told her in a ceremonial voice, 'Run, my dear! Run! And never come back!' And she did. She ran as fast as she could, but she couldn't resist turning back several times. Everybody knows that in those dreams one should never glance back!

She woke up and realized that everything was just a dream, but she was still shaking. And, yes, they were walking, walking and talking and her student is explaining some ideas he had about the wedding party. Step by step, word by word, they walked far out of the village. Now, they are in the middle of the huge ploughed field, with no river to be heard or seen, and no trees around, except one: a big cherry tree, as big as a warrior-oak. And they are heading towards it. She wanted to tell him not to go there, but she knew that he would jokingly dismiss her warnings as superstitious thing of the past. They are in the shade now and her student is glowing with happiness. Above their heads — ripe, in the sudden breeze, sweet cherries are dancing. Her student stretches and picks one and as the fruit breaks between his white teeth the sky opens, a sudden BANG, as when an aircraft breaks the sound barrier and everything after is swallowed by silence. Our teacher is shaking. On succulent summer grass her student is laying dead, with a cherry between his teeth.

So, I was telling her that story and her eyes moistened," continued Victor. "We were walking along the river and there was an orchard on our right side. I pulled the box out and gave her the present. She examined it.

"'It's nice,' she said, and kissed me. Ten minutes after I noticed that she didn't have the box.

"'Where is it?'

"'I don't know.'

She was very surprised. "I must have lost it somehow."

"We retrace our steps and look everywhere. Nada! We both forgot about it. Life pulled us in different directions; decades passed and, guess what? I realized just now how stupid I was. She probably freaked out reading the symbols I mixed. What I was thinking? And I thought that it was a love poem! She must have thrown the box away, thinking that I was trying to hex her! So many years have passed and it still hurts!"

Marko and I uncomfortably listened to the eerie voice behind the door. Sobbing, he kept repeating, "How stupid I was, oh how stupid I was..."

"How strange his memories are!"

"They are no memories," said Mrako, "he never met that girl, never! He was a born soldier, with no time for anything like that. He would only buy love for half an hour. Besides, everything happened before he was born. Philosophy studies had been terminated 200 years ago. It is all madness."

"And it's funny," added Midagar.

The phone rang. A call from hell.

"Northern Guard! This is Commander Mrako Pravica speaking."

"Captain Shaddi speaking.
When my guard falls,
I must be getting calls!"

"I left a message! He's tied up in the confinement room."

"Any other problems you would like to report?"

"Nothing else."

"When a soldier becomes prey,
An exchange is on its way!"

"Yes, Comrade Captain!"

Later, we kissed in the office and the room took off like it was a helico. Everything was getting smaller and smaller and further away...Midagar, Shaddi, Emil, Victor...We were birds. Mrako was rushing high into the sky and I was following. He let me catch up and suddenly left me. I thought every cell in my body was about to explode, but I kept climbing. We reached the spot where breathing became almost impossible and then we descended, gliding in a wide spiral.

"Anya," he says, "I'm lost. I wasn't trained for this."

"We shouldn't talk. Let's not allow words to limit the meaning of what we have."

"No, my dear, I have to talk. The Revolution demands that I remain an ascetic. You are Andrey's sister..."

"We will just be quiet."

"You're flying, Anya! And you fly well! Soon you might become a Hallas!"

We returned to the base.

It was snowing and the helico was landing.

The new guard was stepping out.

The body of the dead guard Victor Troha was brought on board.

The new guardian's name was Finta Maranidra.

12 GENESIS

In the middle of a sand desert
there was a huge white stone.
Male grains jealously commented,
"It's too big, clumsy and ugly!"
while females, fearing the men,
whispered softly to themselves,
"O how strong, white, and tall
he is, how handsome and evil!"

For years the stone paid no heed
to the opinions of the grains,
but one day, when it truly understood,
it got the creeps, cowered and shook,
its greatness turned into powder.
Male grains of sand jealously commented,
"It's an ordinary, poor and incapable dust",
while the girls, fearing the males,
whispered softly,
"Oh how tiny, refined and quiet
he is, how handsome and evil!"

The white powder heard their words,
it got the creeps, cowered and trembled,
but it couldn't turn to anything else.

We stood on the edge of the Zone, facing the desert. The suns would be rising soon. We were barely moving. We chose the end of the night when temperature differences are smallest, when it is very cold in the desert. Schutz, the guardian, didn't see us. We were sure he was sleeping, we chose this area because of that. Emil knew about everything. If necessary, he would cover for us.

Finally, for first time in my life, I stepped on the brown desert sand. I was surprised how hard it was to walk on, like walking on deep wet snow. No wonder the Arijaans are tough! You grow up walking on this in the desert heat?!

Nobody was around and we held hands. Occasionally we kissed gently. A birch tree shimmered in me. The sand drains you. We were walking for an hour and were barely able to stand. Something black started appearing as we went down the dune. An oasis burnt with napalm, the ruins of a village, not much different from the ruins of the cemetery that was next to it. Those tombstones that remained had the shape of birds' heads and were probably painted in their better days. Now it all had the look and smell of charcoal.

Between the ruined walls stood a tall Arijaan. He carried himself as sport superstars do, his worn-out toga looking somehow regal on him. Suns were already up.

"HALT!!!"

"We stopped!"

"The Fish wonders why the water is wet to a dog!"

"A dog wonders about the condor that circles over his master," Mrako replied. Arijaan comes closer. It was Andrey.

"I could see it was you, yet you never know."

"Is everything ready?"

"It is. But you're late!"

Without explanation Andrey walked back to the ruins. He pushed a tombstone and a grave opened like a door. Mrako went after him and, seeing my reluctance, smiled encouragingly. I went down, too. Stooped, following Andrey's flashlight, we walked through the low narrow tunnel.

"It's time for you to become a Hallas," said Andrey.

"She is ready," Mrako confirmed.

I wasn't really sure I wanted to be a Hallas, but it was too late to think about that. Maybe it was more than an urge to save my brother that brought me into this. It looked like there was no end to those underground passages. Andrey would occasionally stop and look at inscribed walls. They were obviously hinting at directions because the network of tunnels was quite complex, more like a labyrinth.

"Did you ever think that you'd walk through these without training? You can't even guess what surprises await you."

"And you know how?" I said with slight irony.

"I do. I am initiated. I am a member of the Action Committee. Only the Action Committee knows the way to the Hallas Temple."

"It sounds selfish to me. Why didn't the Arijaans hide here during the invasion? This looks like a bomb shelter."

"Correct thinking. This is a shelter, but people must never know. For their own good! It's a security issue. When needed, the Committee will let them know."

"And this is the only way that I can become a Hallas?"

"No. Mrako's birth was different. He bumped into a priest or, better put, his body knew where to go and what he wanted. The priest didn't pay any attention to him since he was meditating, but because of that he clearly saw Mrako and his unquestionable desire to go the way of Liberation. Mrako didn't need to be trained by dreams. Life prepared him to become a condor. Your life was different and you had to learn to dream. This war will be merciless, something like a final fight between genetic materials. We have to have our best dogs at the battlefield. Humans will not send ordinary dogs against us. The special forces you heard about are nothing compared with those they are manufacturing now. Their genetic engineers didn't waste time; they are creating a warrior cast by combining the genetic strands of the strong fighting breeds: German Shepherds, Dobermans, Boxers, Borzois, Argentinean Dogos, and who knows what else. Their stamina and aggressiveness are multiplied and their intelligence, according to the information we have, is much higher than ours. They want the new breed to be vastly superior to any existing type of dog. From their point of view, the biggest flow we have comes from the fact that we are mostly randomly mixed. Secretly, between themselves, they call us Strays... and yes, we are physically inferior, we often react emotionally, while the new breed does everything according to cold logic. And you know what I think? — Fuck that! I see it this way: they are ice, but we are fire. The winner will be whoever turns out to be bigger. Either the ice will melt and evaporate, or the fire will be extinguished. What have we got to lose? A life filled with humiliation? Still, the Committee understands the need to improve our force and to utilize the best genetic material we have. Our family genes are strong: one more reason to be here! We'll find out where they are making the new cast of killers. They call them the DOS, which stands for Defenders of the System."

"Anything you can add, Mrako? Why didn't you tell me this before?"

He nodded, shrugged, made same faces..

"You never tell me anything. I always learn about things from Andrey!"

"I can only say what the Committee approved."

"That's right! From now on you'll obey the Committee's decisions. You're ours. There's no way back."

When Andrey was talking, it never crossed my mind to

argue, even when I felt that something was wrong, or disagreed. It's not in accordance with my character, but his authority was indisputable and that was what I started hating.

"What would happen if we chose the wrong passage in this labyrinth?"

"Don't even think about that.

"We're close," said Andrey.

Am I crazy? I mean, he was my brother, but I barely knew him. I had a foggy intuition about Mrako's greatness, but is that the reason that I blindly stuck to whatever they tell me? Where were we going? Was I just a little steel ball in their fanatical pinball of revolution?

"Everybody has to fulfill his or her destiny. Don't have second thoughts," said Andrey. "If you go back the labyrinth would kill you, but we'd never let that happen, we'd kill you ourselves!"

"You would?"

Instead of a "yes," Mrako shrugged. Again.

"Yes, Anya, we'd have to. It's not about you or me or Mrako, it's about the Revolution. But, remember this: if your heart tells you to give up, it is your duty to listen to it, no matter the consequences."

"Let's just go where we're going," I said.

They congratulated me. Andrey said that we were in the Tunnel of the Last Hope. All that was left now was to successfully pass the Challenge. They blindfolded me and walked me into some big room or cave; it was obvious by the echo every sound made. It wasn't cold anymore and the crackling of fire explained why. Hot air! You felt like you were at the seashore in summer. I heard some rhythm, but I couldn't determine what exactly it was. Some hands grabbed my arms, but they weren't Andrey's or Mrako's, some unknown hands. I could now hear only my own steps. It felt like we walked in a circle...or maybe straight... I felt this sudden warmth around my belly button, my mouth was dry, and my steps were becoming quieter even though I tried to walk heavily so the sound would tell me more about where I was. Soon I could not feel anything below my feet though I was clearly walking. Those arms stopped me and placed something like a stone table or cube beneath my feet. It started rotating. My stomach turned so suddenly and violently that I almost puked. The stone I was on was obviously rotating, at first horizontally and clockwise, then vertically and after that pretty much in whichever direction, constantly accelerating. I was glued to it. My skin was itching unpleasantly. Soon, it turned into painful sensation of being pierced by thorns from the inside. I knew that I was blindfolded, but things started appearing before me. I could clearly see the fires all around me. It looked like my own body was burning, too. Some other shapes appeared through flames and then I could see myself from faraway. I was lying in the middle of an amphitheater, surrounded by thousands of old dogs in grey rugged togas, with long silver beards. They waived their bodies and repeated some word rhythmically, something complicated, but at the same time similar to a simple uh-ah-uh-ah sound. The loudness was increasing with every minute and the chanting was speeding up. I felt like something was demanded from me. I didn't know what.

And then, it happened.

The whole room, or cave, expanded suddenly with a deafening hiss. It was like some kind of non-destructive explosion. Above me, huge rocks were circling, whirling unpredictably, sometimes slow, sometimes so fast that I could make out only a blur. I didn't try to figure anything out. I was shocked and paralyzed. The scariest rocks were dark blue, almost black, their razor sharp edges glittering. They rotated all around me, like around a star, but they also rotated around their own axes, just like planets do. The air was full of ozone and breathing felt so empowering . The chanting of the monks had some crispness to it and the universe was in accordance to whatever they were saying. I felt like a goddess. Right above my head a ray of white light appeared, slowly getting closer to me, and widening. Monks repeated their chant in a different tune and I knew I shouldn't wait anymore. They demanded something from me, but what?

My belly button was on fire again and it was spreading all over my body. The stone surface I was laying on somehow kicked and catapulted me. I was flying through the air, spreading and waving my wings feverishly, but gravitation was pulling me down, getting stronger. I had to go up, and beyond up towards the opening that was sending that white light. My bones were grinding, my lungs burning, my vision was getting blurry, but I waved and waved, repeating to myself those same syllables that the monks were chanting. One rock cut my right wing and my feathers fell like snow but I kept going up and up, higher than up, even if my heart burst and my brain fried, I just kept going to where the white light was born. I knew I could do it, I knew I was the best and nobody in the whole universe was as capable as I was. My strength was immeasurable and my endurance challenged the gods who ruled the world of our gods.

Finally, I went through the opening and at that moment something grabbed me and threw me further up. I lost control. Felt like a banana tossed in weird way. Somehow I regained control, spread my wings, and glided through the most wonderful blue light my eyes had ever seen. Not doing anything, just slightly moving my wings, I slowly started to descend. Yes, it was like a reward!

I felt uninhibited.

A at the beginning, my circles were as big as the desert below me, but I was gradually narrowing them. I didn't need crutches of words or ideas. I was free. I could find my way on the shore of all words that were ever spoken. No, it wouldn't be a beach made of rusty iron letters! I could do anything! I could suntan; I could surf on the wild waves or navigate a sail. My mind had no chains. I was not a slave of knowledge.

I noticed a little dot moving on the surface and as I was getting closer to it I could clearly see a Human walking. He had yellow pants, a blue shirt, and a white cloth on his head. He was in a rush. From where he was he could not see mountains and rivers and green fields. Everywhere around him was a desert. From his perspective it looked hopelessly endless and he must find either shade or a well to survive. Every trap functions on the victim's desire to live or to get saved. That's why he was going fast, letting his bodily fluids evaporate, instead of finding any kind of shade and digging himself into the ground and waiting for nightfall. If he could be persistent, walk at night, and follow one strict direction, he could maybe get out of this. However, his chances were small.

I circled above him for hours, and I could see his strength melting like butter on a hot pan. Occasionally, he raised his head and looked at me with fear. I felt no pity. Everybody had somebody who looked at him from above. I could hear him panting, swearing, squealing, and whispering a woman's name, walking slower and slower over the hot desert sand. He tried to keep his moral up. It meant nothing in the desert. Now he ran. He probably believed that he saw an oasis, a meteorology station, a river, or a city! What a disappointment he would have to face when it was not there. Nada! He fell on his knees, sobbing, repeating a woman's name. Then, it looked like he settled his mind, but at the very next moment he was walking on all fours like a baby. Losing his fluids! That was actually good for I was getting tired of this theatre and wanted it to end. His lips were cracked as an overripe fig and sweet Human blood was shyly coming out. My patience was killing him. His fear was pushing him to go on. He couldn't stand the idea of me pecking his flesh, tearing strips off him. He was so used to thinking that almost everything alive was potential food for him. It drove him insane that he could be somebody else's food. Stupid Humans! It was always about somebody else. He couldn't see that even the condor one day faces the moment when he cannot keep himself in the blue of the sky.

The Human fell.

He looked at the sky.

He saw me.

I swiftly dove towards him and before he realized it I had stuck my claws in his chest and with my shiny beak, through his eyes, found the way to his brain.

13 PLAYING DICE

Don't come to my dreams,
Don't wake me every night,
Nothing's as it seems
— The fall is my flight!

The new guard Finta Maranidra sang so loudly that everything shook. His accent was a bit funny, every n he pronounced as n-y, which cheered me up. However, he was anything but a funny guy. He combed his black hair backwards, and his face would probably be beautiful if it didn't constantly express anger and frustration; his eyes looked at you somehow from beneath even though he was tall. He moved like a hyena, like a small town bully's first assistant, unsettled and quiet. Still, I put my arm on the table, rolled up my sleeves and let him work. He was very good.

Sometimes I can't understand you, L.C.," said Mrako.

"I like that."

"That's what I don't understand."

"Why, Comrade Commander?" said Finta. "It will be a beautiful picture! The girls will go crazy over it!"

Mrako smiled, but his eyes were sour.

"You shaved your head, now you tattoo yourself! Interesting, comrade L.C.! I thought you were joking, but it seems to me you're enjoying it. Well, what's life without joy!"

"I am as I am," I said. "I want to be as ugly as a Mongol!"

"Mongol! What's a Mongol?"

"It's an ancient nation from Earth. They weren't particularly ugly, but somebody wrote that they were. You know, this was a quotation."

Finta was showing his perfect white teeth, his smile had a glimmer of deceit.

"You don't care what anybody thinks? You feel uninhibited?"

"Exactly."

"So be it!"

I became a Hallas in a disgusting way: I ate a Human brain. Somehow, when I thought about it I didn't feel any remorse or guilt, but I rather saw it as a form of spiritual cleansing, not savage at all. Next thing I knew, Mrako was waking me up for the change of shift. I asked if everything was just a dream, he said that it really didn't matter anymore and that I had become a Hallas. I didn't ask more, as I knew that he would tell me everything I'd need to know.

The phone was ringing in the office. The guard from Five called to say that he'd spotted a helico. For a couple of minutes the station looked like a madhouse. Everybody was in a rush to sort clothes and boots, clean crumbs from the table, sweep the hall... In no time, it was spotless again.

Captain Shaddi appeared at the door, but the fire picketer stopped him. Mrako signalled to let him in.

"Is Lance Corporal Aganovski here?"

"Yes, he is, Comrade Captain!"

"CALL HIM!"

I felt chills in my spine. Shaddi was the last officer in the world I would want to have any business with.

"Lance Corporal Andrey Aganovski! At your service, Comrade Captain!"

*"Against the wind you don't piss,
Instantly come to the office!"*
Then he added to Mrako,
*"I'll break your every bone
If we are not left alone!"*

The fear left me. Whatever happened I'd do my best, given the situation. If he had uncovered me I would have had to kill him. He wouldn't be that crazy to stay alone with me if he'd known who I was. He offered me a cigarette. We smoked. He grimaced with fake politeness.

"Aganovski, we know that you are one of the best and always have been. You come from an honest and distinguished family that follows the path of the System. I will not beat around the bush. In short, I am offering you to work for me. I have no eyes and ears in this building and you will have to admit that this won't do! We cannot let that happen, for the safety of our people, families, ourselves! Follow what the soldiers do, where they go, what they say and write, and what's going on at our guard posts. This is the honor that you should have received long ago. Your love for the fatherland will be appreciated and rewarded in a proper way. How does this sound to you?"

"Comrade Captain, I see that you think it's easy to be a friend to somebody and then do things behind their back."

"Don't talk nonsense, Aganovski! You know very well that we're in a state of undeclared war. I don't give a flying fuck about minor violations of R 'n' R. Who cares if somebody is hiding a bit of booze, or sweed? Of course, generally speaking, I'm supposed to clamp down on these things, but times are different now and I'm not going to waste my bullets on birds that are so small that you can't even make soup out of them. The enemy is now within. We don't have time for bullshit. Keep an eye on the other corporal and on your commander. Also, keep an eye on Zoran Chitkushev, he's usually on spot Four. There's something fishy about him. Never trust those that read a lot! We're at war. Don't forget that! Internal security is constantly in a state of hyper-alert."

"Comrade Captain, you're saying it in a way that does not leave any doubt that I'd be a traitor if I refused."

"What do you think you'd be? If dogs from families like yours are not with us I don't know what we are doing; we should give up and offer our throats to the Arijaan daggers."

"OK."

"I knew you'd agree. You had to. I guess we're done. I'll yell now for a bit. Don't take it seriously. I'll tell the commander it was about that Arijaan corpse you found in the ice."

As he promised, he started screaming at me and firing all kind of threats. However, as always, his eyes weren't involved, they just constantly evaluated everything, the cold and unsettling eyes of a desert rat. He walked out furiously. The soldiers in the restroom looked shocked and uncomfortable. They were probably thinking, "Aganovski's fucked!" I told them everything that Sahddi had instructed me to say. Everyone was quiet. The hiss of the helico faded. With his eyes, Mrako was asking me what's going on, but in such a careful way that nobody noticed. I winked and remained in the social room. Finta and Taffa were playing dice, Taffa losing and angry, and Emil was teasing him.

"What a stupid dude this corporal Emil is," said Taffa, pretending he was in a good mood. He was known for his short fuse. Emil just laughed as though Taffa had told a really good joke.

"I apologize, comrade corporal," said Taffa. "You're actually not a corporal any more, just a punk, like you always were."

"You're very nervous," Emil replied.

Finta seemed amused, smiling at the soldiers who, lacking any notion of how to make themselves useful, followed the duel.

"Comrades, I think it would be best for the two of them to play and settle it in the game. We don't want anything stupid to happen," Finta said.

"He's probably afraid," said Taffa.

"No problem, I'll play," confirmed Emil in a surprisingly cold voice.

Mrako gave me a signal to go to the office. As soon as we entered he locked the door and embraced me passionately and desperately. He buried his head between my shoulder and neck and deeply inhaled. From the social room we could hear laughter and Taffa's cursing.

"Are you aware what we are into?" Mrako said gently."

"Yes, I am."

"Our relationship is unacceptable. A Hallas revolutionary doesn't fall in love. Love is for the Big Battle as they say; it doesn't leave space for this kind of love. Love is possible only between free people and this kind of love is something that weakens our fighting spirit. Therefore it's subversive and works to the gain of the enemy."

"Do you guys always talk in this state of uninhibited feeling?"

"It's not... You have it while you're a condor in the sky. The Condor teaches you freedom, but you, as a dog-Hallas, have to conquer that freedom on the ground. That's why the Committee says that the illusion of love confuses the warrior's notion of being already dead."

"Mrako, I'll tell you openly, I don't think I can have any spirit without you."

With an expression of condolence and compassion he petted my bald skull. For the first time I felt embarrassed and sorry about my lack of hair.

"What did Shaddi want?"

"To have me rat for him."

"You agreed?"

"I did, supposedly."

"He loves misty games. Heaven, how gentle your breasts are!"

My chest was covered. It was never big, anyway. In his arms, I had no doubt, I was a bitch. I had no trouble acting and feeling like a man, I even found some joy in the military way of life. First of all, you have to be your own best friend; it would be devastating if you had any doubt about it. Your life is so miserable that you have to appreciate things you barely noticed before: a good sleep or a meal, clouds in the sunset, a beautiful tree frosted over with ice. You learn how to communicate on different levels and to always do what suits you best. That was my experience. Regarding Mrako, I had no doubts; I couldn't see any misunderstanding arising between us. We can overcome anything, my mixed-breed and me.

In the soc-room some shit was going on. You could hear Taffa's mean swearing, yelling at soldiers, and violent banging of furniture, fists at work. Mrako ran in.

"Freeze!"

Everybody stopped except Taffa and Emil who were wrestling on the floor. Soldiers had lots of trouble separating them. Even then they wanted to hit each other and Mrako had to dish out punches to both of them. In the situation, the only happy person was Midagar, who was obviously enjoying it.

"Midagar, Emil, Andrey — to the office! Djordjevic, you stop Taffa's bleeding. OK, good! Everybody out, now!"

I'd never seen Mrako so angry. All the soldiers came in front of the guardhouse, some of them in slippers and pyjamas, or whatever the moment caught them in. We knew how cold it was outside and three of us felt some stupid joy that our ranks gave us some protection from this kind of punishment. The soldiers had to do push-ups.

"32, 33..."

When they were done their heads were smoking, their red noses running, the sweat and snot stuck to them. Their limbs and faces were blue.

"Don't you think you went too far?" asked Midagar, this time without his cynical grin.

"No! While I'm commander here there will be discipline. Emil and Taffa will have to defer to superior rank. And you, if you're so interested..."

"What? You'd fuck me too?"

"I wouldn't exclude that option."

"I always knew you were a faggot."

Mrako grabbed his neck and pushed him against the wall, lifting him in the air. Midagar looked like a rag doll, obviously choking.

"That was a preview," Mrako said, releasing him.

Midagar tried to fashion his famous grin, but he was shaking and had trouble breathing.

14 SQUATTING IN THE FOG

"I understand, Anya, everything's clear to me. You're on the other side. I was considering reporting all of you. You're dragging our name through the mud, but… you know very well I couldn't do it. You destroyed my life. Yours, too. And mother's."

"Dad, there's no going back, but I want you to know that I've always loved you and nothing can change that. We might be on opposite sides, but we will never fight each other. That's what I think. It was destiny that things panned out as they did."

"Destiny, fate, that is what you guys always talk about. It's easy to destroy! Try making something! If you ever win you'll see what you'll turn into, how quickly high ideals lapse to the lowest common denominator. Just go away, Anya! Go! May luck be with you, but don't ever come back to this house!"

I walked out of everything I was. From now on my home would be my boots.

At the base, the atmosphere was normal, those that were to go on shift yelled and made all kinds of commotion, those who wanted to sleep complained, begged, threatened .

Mrako was sitting with his feet on the desk, smoking.

"Midagar asked where you were."

"Did you tell him anything?"

"I told him to look after his own duties and that you were on an assignment."

"Only that?"

"Only that. Tell Shaddi that I sent you to No. 4 to spy on Krasha. Report that he smoked and sat. He always does that. Say that you have a strong feeling something is going on and that Krasha might be involved, but that you cannot determine what it is. That he is acting strange, like he's plotting something. They will fuck with Krasha a bit, they might even catch him bringing in sweed, but nothing will happen beyond some solitary and some bathroom detail."

"What kind of game is Shaddi playing?"

"Can't say. He's up to something. We should be careful. Both sides are preparing to strike."

"You have information?"

"No. I need no information. It's been brewing for so long. The Committee doesn't waste time, be sure about that."

"When will I meet the members of the Committee?"

"I don't know. I know only one."

"Andrey!"

"Only him."

Midagar brought the second shift back. While he was putting ammo in the safe he was looking at me pretending he knew something. I acted as if I didn't notice. My duty was starting soon and if no overseer came I'd have an hour to take a nap. It was against Rules and Regulations, but I was dead tired. I waited for Midagar to go to bed and grabbed the key to Solitary. What a paradise! To be alone in a room is everybody's wish! Lying there, I thought about Mrako, imagining him being next to me.

The solka had been empty since Victor died. I was on the same bed, and not even the sheets had been changed. It didn't make it uncomfortable, I was just aware of it. Mrako would not come, the fire picketer was in the hall. Just thinking of Mrako spread sweet warmth through me, like wine. I was dozing in that gentle reverie, but very soon a horrible picture crept into my soul. My mixed breed and I are making love, but somebody is screaming outside. I look out and I see my Dad and Mom being slaughtered by factory workers. That was like getting a punch in the stomach while you're tanning on the beach with your eyes closed. I went back to the office, washed my face, made coffee. I was nervous. Mrako said nothing, like he already knew everything. It was time for the change of shift.

"C'mon soldiers, wake up! Getting fat at the people's expense! Get the fuck out of those beds you bunch of stinky snails!" I am kicking their beds and what I say I really mean at the moment.

"Easy, easy!" Emil said.

"I'm sorry! I feel like shit."

Some nights are different than others and you crave sleep more. Like a bunch of moonwalkers we slouched to the earthwork, and then boarded the helico. It left the ground like a drunken dragonfly. Soldiers yelled from the cage. The pilot was new, stiff, and quiet. The helico was bouncing in the air like a car racing through the bushes. I warned the pilot to be careful. We almost hit a tree while landing on Five. When he finally managed to get the aircraft down I decided to continue on foot and ordered the pilot back to base. That night didn't like us: a cold, badly trained pilot, long walks from post to post.

When I was done with the changing of the guard the idiot was still circling above Five like he had forgotten how to navigate. The help was supposed to be there already, instead of that we got fireworks: the helico exploded in the air.

At the base, I quickly wrote my report and went to bed. Mrako would check the ammo and store cartridges for me.

I wasn't asleep for more than five minutes when they woke me up. A soldier from One had heard screams coming from Eight. I had to go, but we didn't have a helico! I chose Babic and Lichina to go with me. We took a motor sleigh and prayed that the old piece of junk would make it. It died half way there. Somebody from higher command was fiddling with expense numbers that look good on paper at the end of the year. Like every other asshole, he dreamed of promotion.

Mrako will come with sergeant Arbut, Shaddi's assistant, who will conduct an investigation. We have to walk. We are advancing over frozen snow that scrunches under our boots. When we arrive at 8 all is quiet. Too quiet. Nobody is stopping us and I already have a bad feeling regarding Emil, who guarded this post. I call him. No reply. We walk around and finally Lichina finds him on the ground. He was killed with an improvised spear, a sharpened tree branch, his hands around it, like he had tried to grab it or pull it out. The murderer obviously approached him from the front. Emil must have known him for he'd never let anybody come that close. How had the mysterious visitor got the spear brought his spear? Maybe he had it hidden under his long coat or simply covered the sharpened end, making Emil think it was one of those improvised walking sticks that shepherds often use. It was clear to me that Emil was not killed by an Arijaan, but by a military person, likely a fellow guardian. Arbut, the unbelievably stupid looker, wrote down some of my conclusions to have something for the file. I say that because it was obvious that he wasn't interested, which made me conclude that Shaddi could be behind this. Arbut was a bad actor.

Mrako was not saying anything. Midagar was nagging. He would like to accuse Mrako, but he was afraid to. Mrako didn't say a word the whole night.

At dawn, Shaddi stormed the building with a squad of military police. Without warning, they went directly to

Taffa's bed and dragged him down. Still asleep, he fell from the second level. Four of them were kicking him! Taffa looked like he didn't understand anything.

"His fingertips were on the stick!" screamed Shaddi.

"Comrades, the stick is mine, but I didn't do it! I swear on my mother's grave! I cut it for hunting jumping porcupines during the shift! Thought I could make some money! I didn't kill Emil! I didn't kill Emil Borucinsky!"

They shot him on our bedroom floor. The helico pilot, Emil and Taffa — three "casualties" in one night!

"It's always a piece of cake
to kill a treacherous snake!" said Shaddi.

For several days Mrako remained silent. Time dragging, and there was a sense of spooky anticipation. Midagar and two soldiers, Finta and Cuffay, claimed that somebody shot at them from bushes.

"Arijaans!" the soldiers hissed with hate and fear.

Finally, when we were alone, Mrako opened his mouth, "Don't trust anybody. Shaddi jump-started a complicated game. The helico pilot was the officer of State Security. At least, so the Committee said. You almost crashed with him. That death and everything else that happened later we can read in different ways. One thing I am sure about is that in this puppet theatre Shaddi is pulling strings. What's his game? Certainly, we're in danger. I'm afraid to question information that the Committee provided about the helico pilot. It doesn't make sense for Shaddi to kill him; I don't think he would ever kill a National Security officer. Does it mean that the Committee lied to us? If it did, we should have been dead. If they knew about us they would have neutralized us. I want you to know that I violated Revolutionaries' Code. I never reported to the Committee my fondness for you, nor asked them for forgiveness. I knew they would say that it was a bad time for our marriage and that Liberation and Revolution need me. Another thing, even worse than that: you are Andrey's sister and he's my blood brother, plus my fellow Hallas. My connection to you is half-incestuous. I'm afraid we don't have much of a chance. I'm sorry. I need you. More than ever. A Hallas is not supposed to need anything or anybody. Freedom is his lover. For them, I've lost my honor. I want you to know: I love you."

I'm listening; whatever I wanted to say got stuck in my throat. Mrako continued, as though in a trance:

"And why did that helico explode? Why would Shaddi sacrifice one of his own? Maybe he's suspecting you of being a Hallas. But what if he knew? With the helico explosion he would kill both Emil and you, but also a bunch of soldiers unrelated to his task. Not to mention how much trouble it would be for him. Maybe his aim was to isolate me. However I tried to analyze it, nothing made sense. Still, there is one possibility. None of his guys is dead and one of ours is. He gave you corporal duties and you'll be promoted soon. He demoted Emil and then Emil got killed. I think he only has half the information or a good guess, but he's biding his time, waiting for us to make a move."

I just let Mrako talk, without interrupting. He seemed to be thinking out loud.

"Let's say that he thinks that you're Andrey. If he killed you, there would be a full investigation into the death of a young officer, and the son of a respected businessman and politician. Now, investigations dredge up all kind of things. No one wants an investigation. Since your father is powerful enough, Shaddi doesn't want to risk anything. He wants to be sure, otherwise he could be court-martialed himself for taking the law in his own hands and circumventing due process. I doubt that his superiors know anything about any of this. You see, that's why he chose Emil. It was not unheard of for a corporal to be demoted. When a corporal dies, since it's still a rank, even if it's the lowest, the big brass must investigate. When a soldier dies,

Shaddi conducts the investigation. Besides, who but you, me, and Andrey would give a fuck about Emil's death? Like me, he comes from a line of social nobodies. Emil had no family to start asking questions. Even for the Committee, Emil is just four letters in Andrey's reports."

I looked at my recent tattoo. Mrako caught that.

"Taffa didn't do it, he said. However temperamental he was, he was a good person. So..."

"You think it was Finta?"

"Why not? He sparked the fight between Emil and Taffa, he wanted it. Even if Taffa killed Emil, which I find unlikely, I would imagine that it was actually Finta's plan. Frankly, it's too fishy, the scenario is too transparent. I think Finta himself did the job. I also think that Shaddi is letting us figure some things out. That is part of his game."

"How can you be so sure that Shaddi thinks that I'm Andrey?"

"Because otherwise he would legally be entitled to kill you on the spot. Anyone infiltrating the service, according to the Rules and Regulations, should be eliminated. Shaddi makes one real move, and then he bluffs a couple of times. He wants to see what happens next."

"Why don't we kill him?"

"We could, but we must know what we will gain by that. Shaddi has set several traps and now he's just waiting. He's hoping we'll get ensnared, floundering in all that fog that he's manufactured. Well, I say we do nothing. Let's just squat in this fog and wait."

"Do you think it's possible that the Committee is partly behind this?"

"I've already said I wouldn't rule that out. But if they knew about us, they'd sanction it."

"I don't think the Committee is involved."

"We mustn't trust anybody."

"So, what do we do?"

"I told you. Nothing. Just follow your instincts. Forget

about the Human part of you."

I put my head on his shoulder. His arm was around me. His smell was intense and had a new nuance to it, an odor of sheep in addition to his regular one. I now know it's the smell of fear. He wasn't scared for his own safety. He was afraid for me. A Hallas who was afraid? I know it's not supposed to be, but that's what we were. According to the Codex of Aja-Hall it was love that prevented us from becoming Divine Warriors.

It looked like the engineers at the Institute for Climate Control had some surprises, it was -60 outside.

I caught a cat
A cat

I ripped it open
Took out guts
Her guts

I put my soul inside
My soul
And I sewed her

Now
she's rambling the world
dying of hunger

15 DEAD SOLDIERS LOVE TO STAND GUARD

Mrako said I should wait at the Morning Star. The jasper in black was laughing his ass off. He acted as though the very sight of me was incredibly funny. I shoved a couple of bills in his pocket, but he refused to take them.

"I don't want them," he said. "I only want to observe you! It's so entertaining!" I kicked him in the crotch. He reeled on the floor, screaming without a sound.

"You fucking animal!" he said.

"Why? Isn't it funny? I find it amusing!"

"What the fuck do you want?" he mumbled, my boot on his forehead.

"Nothing. I'm here for fun. And that's you!"

"Leave me alone."

"Why should I? Everybody likes a bit of fun. Do you know any songs?"

"Songs?"

"Do you know that song, 'How the Morning Star is Connected to Arijaans'?"

He said nothing. I shifted my foot to his neck and

pressed the fucker. His eyes bulged.

"KKKhhh. OK! I'll sing, I'll sing..."

"I'm waiting."

He started:

"Solnchentze zahaya

Invas tiho spi,

Lunitza prihaya

Ptichek dzvrgolyi!"

I smashed his nose. He was bleeding.

"Connected, connected, connected....we are just an entertainment facility... you see....and.... think about it, where the dogs are sovereign? Where there are no Humans, you see... in the desert there are no Humans. And none in Rabbat either, understand?"

"What do you know about my visits here?"

"I only know that you visit."

"Do you know why I always have to come here?"

"For security reasons! What better place can you find in Chortwille?"

"Why did those German shepherds attack me?"

"It was an accident. They were defenders of the system, you see – they're dogs, too. They also like to have fun, but we can't deny them entrance. You shouldn't complain. We spent lots of money greasing the machine, so they don't clamp down on us."

I could have gleefully cut his throat.

"Who's the owner?"

"I don't know."

I grabbed his balls and squeezed. His face turned greyish-blue, the vein on his forehead thick as a thumb.

"I'm waiting."

"The Commi..."

"Yes, 'commi,' just fucking say it!"

"Commi....tteee..."

He was a clown that was not funny, an actor who was not convincing in his role. He begged me not to tell anyone about that. I promised. I was sure he'd keep his mouth shut. I descended those famous stairs to the middle of the dance floor and chose a table in the darkest corner.

Andrey was supposed to come. We always waited for him. Andrey was so serious. He never joked. He was a Hallas, a Divine Fucking Warrior. What was wrong with me? I used to enjoy humor and harmless pranks so much and it was all gone now. The end of childhood, I guessed. I was sure once there was no humor the world's illusions ossify, turn to armor, and the growth stops. I've read that Humans on Earth used to force girls to wear some kind of wooden shoes so that their feet would stop developing and remain so small that it would forever prevent them from walking normally. This was considered very distinguished and beautiful! So much suffering just for a vision of beauty, for prestige! It was all bullshit. Andrey was bullshit, too. He was no better than father; actually, it was clear that he was worse. This is the twisted part: I didn't regret being a Hallas, or something like that. I was a condor or something like that. The one who quenches his thirst with heavenly heights has enough stamina to walk through hell. And I am in hell.

This time the atmosphere in the Morning Star was pleasant, more ordinary. Two couples danced dreamily to some old ballad. A wiry guy was watering himself with pink tequila. I had a double vodka on ice. Like a rock star, getting down on the podium, Andrey finally arrived. He was in a good mood.

"We're always waiting for you."

"I'm sorry, but it couldn't be any different."

"It got complicated at the base. I don't know how much you've been following, but we think that Shaddi is trying something."

"Don't worry about that. We are watching Shaddi. You can have full confidence in the efficiency of our orders. You're safe. Certainly, a condor always has to be on alert."

"Condor, condor... Safe! You know that Emil's dead?"

"I know. Don't ask me about it. You're safe. How safe are they with condors around?"

"Condor, condor! Have you ever seen one, the real one?"

"Of course I haven't. They lived long ago. Because of some mutations they were bigger than those on Earth; you can find a picture in the central library. Nobody knows how they went extinct. Some claim that condors still exist in the Torich Mountains. I'd say if they're extinct they just evolved from a lower to a higher form of existence. The dusha of Hallas is the condor's home. I'm not here to have scholarly discussions. You and Mrako are to receive the honor of getting a special assignment. Remember what I'm saying. Don't talk. Listen. There is a hospital for children in Human core of Chortville. They have a Laboratory for Genetic Improvements in its basement. The truth is: it's a disguised military company. We don't know how far they have advanced with their research, but according to the information we have they are preparing version 7.5.1 of Defender of the System. That would be the new superior dog race I told you about. They are not only physically or intellectually superior to us, but—and this is the most up-to-date intel—they are supposed to have paranormal abilities. What that would be, we have no idea. Mrako and you are to destroy all the prototypes you find there. Don't worry. They should still be at the most basic level. There was a fatal bug in a previous version, but this was never published. Supposedly, they killed some scientists and a whole generation was recycled into fertilizer. So, the task is clear. You have to neutralize all of them and destroy everything else in there. They, for sure, have a backup somewhere, but at least we'll slow them down enough. It's up to you and Mrako how you'll do it. Try to stay alive. If you have no choice don't even think of dying without completing the mission!"

"So... Kill them all?"

"All."

"I will pass the message on. How much time we got?"

"Two days."

"OK. It's an honor. Look, I want to ask you about something else..."

"Yes?"

"Our parents, why are you being so rude to them?"

"I'm not. It might seem so to you, but it's not."

"Maybe..."

"Anya, you are a Hallas! Can't you understand another Hallas? A Hallas has only one real love, holy love — Revolution!"

I left the Star depressed. With a drink in his hand, wearing an expensive suit, Andrey looked like a playboy from some upper-class resort.

At the base, they were waiting for replacements. Three new guards still hadn't arrived. I told Mrako everything about the Morning Star, orders of the Committee, information about Shaddi. Lots of news.

"And again — we know nothing. They want to sacrifice us? Is the diversion real? You know what, let's not over-analyze; let's just do as they say. If the Committee thinks so…"

"You think we really should die? Is that what you mean?"

"It is. I cannot change my skin."

"Ever thought about going somewhere far away, creating a new identity?"

"No. For a Hallas every destiny is good except losing one's honor... because..."

The noise of the landing helico swallowed his words. Three soldiers jumped out from the cage platform. Captain Shaddi emerged from the cockpit. Midagar was already there to greet his favorite officer, but he quickly came back white as a corpse, shaking slightly.

"Victor!"

"Victor? What do you mean?"

Midagar just passed by, saying nothing. He locked himself in the bathroom. Shaddi came.

"Any problems?" he said cheerfully.

"No, Comrade Captain! All problems are now fixed with these new soldiers!"

"Excellent! Love to hear that. Since there are no problems I think I am not really needed here!" He jumped on board and the helico swiftly left.

Silence. Everybody was quite shocked with the arrival of three new guys. They approached us carefully and sheepishly, as new soldiers always do. One face we knew very well from before, Victor Troha. If there was one around, you would probably hear a mosquito in the air. Two other guys were nervously sweating, just like us. The only one who was calm, but somehow out of place, was Victor.

"Aganovski, show these soldiers their beds and slots for their rifles!" said Mrako.

"I serve the people, Comrade Commander!" I said, but I didn't leave, waiting to hear the story.

"We thought you were dead," said Mrako. "You actually were dead."

"I know. I kind of remember some chaotic pictures, a jumping porcupine, even being dead." said Victor. "You wake up, but you don't know any more who you are. They had to teach me who I was. I'm so happy to be home again."

In a second, everybody was in the soc room around Victor. He looked lost and embarrassed, like when a modest person suddenly becomes a celebrity. The soldiers had hundreds of questions; some of them quite stupid (like, "Do you still get morning wood?"). He was answering patiently with a smile that tried to hide enormous internal pain and confusion. Looking at him didn't give you much comfort; I mean he was as pale as a corpse. Supposedly, using some new techniques, they reanimated him and even succeeded in regenerating some dead brain tissue. Some stiffness in his movements proved that the power of science is not unlimited.

"You kept mentioning some pancakes or crepes!" said Midagar, laughing.

Victor covered his face with his hands and started crying.

"Please, please, never ever mention that. Nobody can cope with it. You don't know what it is, I beg you all: Never remind me of that!"

Everybody was quiet. Mrako said that we all heard what Victor just said. We must never talk about that.

"They did save me," said Victor like a shy village girl, "but not without consequences."

Mrako didn't have to threaten anyone, for every soldier in the room, even the biggest asshole, was deeply touched and felt strong compassion for their peer.

Outside, in the mean cold of the Zone, the wind was whistling. The soldiers from the mountains believed it was the weeping of lost souls.

Mrako still hadn't decided when we would go to "smash scions." It was my time for the shift.

16 FIRE

Fire, fire, fire will come,
Cities will scream in flame,
Freedom cannot be undone
— Nothing will stay the same!

Maggots drop from every nose
And the Dead are now alive
— The Soul of the Warrior arose,
In heaven you will dive!

Walk tall under the stars
And stop this life of shame;
In battle earn your scars,
Eternal will be your fame!

May grass be your hair,
May rain wash your face,
You are what you dare
For Freedom and the Race!

17 SCIONS

You didn't know anymore who you can trust. The confidence I had in Mrako helped me overcome the fact that I should not believe my own brother. They were showing us a film for "entertainment and relaxation," one of those adaptations of Human novels, but in a so-called dog-version. It was about a guy who was travelling on the train and couldn't sleep. There was a femme-fatale blonde dressed in black, walking in the aisle. They talk. They have some vodka etc. Now, they are at some seashore resort. He has a dream that the special police were after him and tells her about it.

"Maybe it wasn't a dream," she says. "They're after me."

He tries to get rid of her, but she's extremely hurt, cries and uses all kinds of tricks. Through the cheesy development of the story she turns him into her sexual and financial slave. Surprisingly, it becomes a porn film. The soldiers were delighted. I looked at Victor, he had a painful expression. Mrako gave up on the film and left the room.

Life here was organized in a way that didn't let you think about anything. We didn't want stupid films to distract us from ourselves and the assignment. Tonight, we were going on a mission to destroy scions. Mrako came back during the third showing. He went to meet a courier. A fierce fight had already started in the Eastern Zone. The Movement had no time to give more precise instructions. "There is an assignment! There is a time frame! Use your vision!"

Again, they copulate on the screen. For a brief moment, Mrako slightly touched my finger. How sweet it was!

"Let's fly!" he said in the office.

I shrank in the corner. He closed his eyes, resting his forehead on the cold wall. We let our condors take over. I am a whirlpool and I am falling into that same whirlpool. There is an icy stone platform at the bottom and I bounce off it.

I fly. Drops of water are falling off my wings; the air is filling my lungs, calming me. Mrako leads. We fly almost vertically, towards the bigger Sun, the "Bread-Sun." In my head, I can hear that radio voice from before with lots of interference.

"Hello, grandsons,
Who will die as I did!
I kissed the fire, I hugged the sea,
I let suns teach me my darkness!
With every breath you take,
I am reborn!
When you laugh, I laugh in you!
And all the mountains sing my song
And the death is a place to be!"

Who transmitted this message was not important to me. I knew that future events would be less poetic. Bitches would scream naked and in blood. Males would creep on the ground with their stumps bleeding. They would be deliberately hitting walls with their skulls to escape the pain and humiliation, to fly, to fly fearlessly into the Bread-Sun that shines like a helmet of the warrior.

Strong scent of menthol.

Our wings are stronger than ever.

It is getting unbelievably hot and we have to turn back. With wings flat against the body, at high speed, we are diving down.

"The Condor can fly directly into Bread-Sun. The passage opens to him. That is the final act of determination."

"And will he burn?"

"Yes, he will burn. That is when the colors are born."

The ground is rapidly approaching our beaks. Spiky, stony mountains point their spears at us.

"A Hallas gives himself up, sacrificing everything he has."

We spread our wings and stop diving, drawing circles on the sky above the mountains. Deserts and cities, cities, and deserts lay in the distance. The radio voice continues in a clear reverb-whisper:

You wonder what haunts you,
What itches your soul.

I say:
The dream-breaker in your chest,
Blind as a puppy,
Digs through your insides,
Widens his home,
His cave of hope and moss.

You wonder how and what,
What should you do?

I say:
A shiny dagger find,
Let many ears grow on it
And when it hears a constant beat,

Stab! Stab! And kill!
That's where he hides!

Raise your head, look in my eyes!
Obey the wisdom, walk on my path!
That's me, your stolen childhood,
With lips bent in a boat!

18 DIVERSION

We entered the Human circle much easier than we expected. Midagar thought that we are on a mission to set a trap for the phantom Arijaan who'd been provoking the guard for a few nights. It was a hoax Mrako and I had concocted using a soldier who was often delusional, but whose discoveries we pretended to believe in, so we could use it one day.

The night's darkness only partially protected us. The Core of Superiors of Freedom was lit by those expensive archaic lamps called "Moonlight." They provide visibility, but don't disturb Human sleep. It was hard to think they wouldn't notice us, but Mrako had quite a good idea what we needed to do. Since we are shorter than Humans, he figured out that we could use popular masks that were memorabilia of the legendary TV series The Last Pirate of the Galaxy. With them and cheap gloves that made our palms look Human he ensured that to any security camera we'd seem like Human kids, kids who are having some harmless fun. First thing we did in the Core was to set off fireworks and then run. Mrako wanted the authorities to notice us. Then we did a bunch of other things kids would do. We threw pebbles at a window and ran, smoked in the park, climbed a tree to steal sweet cherries, etc. It took a while. Then we acted tired and just walked the streets. Nobody had reacted, which meant that we were safe. I was impressed with Mrako's idea for it gave us lots of opportunities to search the Core because we had a very foggy concept of where the location would be.

The impression that the Human circle made on me was magnificent. I'd never seen anything so beautiful. Big family houses with gardens I could never possibly imagine existed, an eternal mild summer and a breeze that spread the scent of roses and unknown herbs, fountains and ponds, water lilies and bindweed, and exotic, mysterious arbors. The smell of tasty meals wafting from windows and the sounds of the families that lived there — it made you think that this must be the most peaceful species in the universe — pure refinement and richness. At one terrace, we spotted a man and a woman petting each other. He was around 40, she a bit younger, both of them well groomed and dressed. They sat on a yellow wicker sofa. He whispered something in her ear and she smiled. His fingers went through her rich wavy hair, patted her shoulders and waist, and he kissed her cheeks and lips and unbuttoned the top of her shirt. The voice of a child came from within the house, they both stopped, startled, and we saw a five-year-old coming to sit between them. It was probably a boy with long black hair but it could have been a girl. The father kissed the child and mother started singing some Human song about a fawn that had lost its herd and was wandering through icy woods looking for them. It snowed and wolves were howling. You could see a tear in the kid's eye. The father grabbed him and hoisted him in the air. The kid laughed. Mrako, surprised himself by what we saw, touched my shoulder letting me know that we had to go. Information about location of the kid's hospital was not accurate at all.

We found it almost by accident. A small white building

surrounded with flowers. We thought it would be very hard to get into, but it had no special security on the outside. Closer observation caused more of a shock. At the back of the building in the shadow cast by a big oak tree, there was a half-open window and two obsolete security cameras that gave us an almost 15-second time-frame to get in unnoticed! I could see what Mrako called "the Human superiority complex." It obviously never crossed their mind to protect the object better. We walked around the block again and came in at the back of the building. Mrako entered first, and then, after the signal, I followed. We didn't have any special equipment, just guns, knives, and ropes. Disalarming the place was a joke! Stupid Humans! We entered a room full of washed pyjamas that obviously had dropped down from the laundry chute. Mrako put a finger to my mouth and I surprised myself by doing something inappropriate, I licked his finger. He laughed soundlessly, grabbed me, and gave me a long sweet kiss. There was nothing in this room but a kid's pyjamas and us. I tickled him. He pulled me to the floor, touching me everywhere.

"I am a virgin," I said sheepishly, like I'm acting in one of those afternoon TV series for professional housewives.

"My little bitch," said he, "you won't be much longer."

And so it was.

In the middle of the Core, time was running against us. We sneaked out to the hall. The security guard was sleeping with his head on a sports magazine. Again, no special measures anywhere! We walked down into the basement. It smelled of mildew. A morgue with fridges for "little Humans," a storage room with discarded miniature beds… Was this a trap? We stood confused. The Condors in us were hastily searching for the solution. I opened the door of an old closet. It hid another door, armored like those of bank safes. Unbelievable! Like in adventure books!

How did we get in? Did the Committee decide to send

us here just to get us killed? Why didn't they provide us with more information? Mrako was trying to find the combination to open the safe. How stupid it was! We were stuck! A couple of hours passed before we heard somebody's steps. It was the security guy; he didn't turn any lights on, but used his flashlight. That helped.

Now, we could see what the secret of the door was. It was a facade and there was no right combination of numbers. Instead, he said something in a language unknown to us, probably one of those Earthly proto-languages. It sounded like poetry, and even though I had never heard it before I could not shake the feeling that I had grown up with it, that it was mother's milk translated in words. I thought I remembered it, maybe because I was just reminded.

> *"Ja nadyoh izvor bayan*
> *u krshnoj, divlyoy gori.*
> *Tu potok vedro-syayan*
> *planinski strah zhubori.*
> *U granyu ptitze tyute.*
> *Sve bilyke ko u tuzi.*
> *Po hladnoy gorskoy steni,*
> *gle, crna zmiya puzi..."*

> (I found a magic spring
> on a wild mountain
> where a glittery creek
> whispers wilderness' s fear.
> The birds are quiet.
> The plants are mourning.
> On the cold cliff
> the black snake slivers…)
>   Yovan Grchich Milenko, Earth, 19th century

When he finished, the door opened by simply

disappearing like it was never there. That was impressive! As soon as the guy stepped in, Mrako whistled. The Human turned. Mrako had to jump very high to stick the knife in his chest. The guard fell like a sack of potatoes. We hastily walked into a big room full of incubators, a room with one half painted black, the other painted yellow. On the black side there was a sign: DEAD – REVIVAL; on the yellow side it said EMBRYO.

On the left, black side, there were bodies of adult dogs, connected with wires and tubes to some kind of medical equipment. We saw Taffa's corpse. It was clear how it was possible that the helico pilot died in such a stupid way. Shaddi would never sacrifice his officer, unless he was already dead. So the pilot we saw was not the real old him, but a synthetic zombie-defender with flows and bugs in his code. Victor wasn't real. Well, a part of him actually was.

In the EMBRYO section we could see children, all of them the same age, maybe two-year-olds. They were to be a new breed of defenders. All the incubators were connected to the same bio-computer that was probably programming them while they were on the fast-growing track.

Then a loud bang from a rifle surprised us. Mrako fell to the ground. The security guy obviously didn't die. I cut his knee, and when he bent forward in pain I jumped up and slit his throat.

I was already crying when Mrako opened his eyes. He was just scratched. As I stubbed the bio-computer, all the bodies, both adults and babies, started screaming. What a noise! Like a sound of thousands of rats being skinned alive. Mrako poured rubbing alcohol over the computer and set the place on fire. From the Human's rifle he sprayed bodies. There was blood everywhere. Blood and fire.

We're running through gardens and backyards. Police is on the streets. We can hear sirens of emergency trucks fated to be late.

IN THE BASEMENT

Treacherously, from behind,
somebody stubs him.
Or maybe the cello hurts?
The cello hurts.

Nastasia sobs
and through the basement window
observes human feet.

The day is ending
in a crumpled tablecloth.

He sings about journeys to the East,
about Rabbat and flowers,
a raven that talks
and a chance to achieve something.

On the squeaky army bed,
skinny and small, coughed a Sunshine.
"That road is covered
with bulgy canine eyes,
tenderness hides in there!"
says he.

Nastasia still sobs.
She knows too well
the scent of basement flowers
And a gutter.
A sweet and a dark gutter.

19 IN BED

Stan Sever is known for his love of singing folk songs, but his most famous feature is snoring. He simply blew away any hope you might have had about sleep. He was one of two soldiers who came with Victor as a replacement. If it felt that somebody in the bedroom was trying to cut metal tubes with a hacksaw, you could be sure Stan Sever was not on duty. It didn't take long until everybody was pissed off with him. If you saw a soldier with big black shadows around his eyes then it was obvious that he was on Sever's shift. In fact, nobody used the term second shift any more. Sever's shift! I was giving up on sleep, sinking in my moist thoughts. That old feeling was in my chest: somebody was tuning up a guitar, picking the strings. I breathed slowly and deeply, hoping that it would alter my mood. I was pretending I was asleep, I didn't want to talk to anybody, like the slightest communication could smash me. I thought that such moments would be gone once I became a Hallas. Mistake. Not even condors are spared from sorrow. The old feeling of being useless pushed me to the edge of reality. There was nothing there.

I could hear soldiers whispering. They were putting

pieces of paper between Sever's toes. They set them on fire. Stan Sever "rides the bicycle". Stan Sever wakes up. Stan Sever swears. Stan Sever spits on his fingers and moisturizes burnt spots. Stan Sever turns on the other side. Stan Sever snores!

Until yesterday the world looked to me like a nice place. Only occasionally something bad would happen, to save us from dying of boredom. And suddenly — what? Condors! Guard! Revolution! The ground under my feet tilted! And everything that was stable was sliding into an abyss!

Andrey said that operation "Smashing the Scions" was a complete success and that Mrako and I qualify for the People's Hero medal. The People's Hero medal? I had never heard of that before.

"This operation," said he, "was a prerequisite for the success of all moves we will make in the time to come. Their project is at least slowed down. We should not wait for them to complete it! It could be fatal. We have to take the initiative and launch the offensive."

He never mentioned reuse of the dead, but we guessed that he knew more. What if Shaddi worked for Andrey? We would play dumb. At least we were aware that we should be careful regarding Finta, Victor, and Midagar. We won't make a move, we will squat in the fog and wait. I'd be happy to sleep and escape this place for a moment. No way. It was lucky that I could blame everything on Stan Sever.

The longing was taking me over, the longing for a breakfast that our servant Rose always brought with a smile, for my mother's criticism, for father's jokes when he returned from the business meeting that finished earlier. My good old bed, my music collection and books— those days are gone forever. The hand of fate was throwing us like dice.

Thirty of us sleep in this room, thirty "comrades," but only regarding five of them could you be sure they wouldn't kill you in your sleep. You live with that, and that becomes ordinary. You didn't think of it. It happened to somebody else. You just slept if you could.

I see no perspective.

The horizon became narrow.

This planet is lost.

Everything is wrong.

Desperation gives birth to another desperation.

There is nothing to be won.

At the end there will be desperation.

When Victor was dying from porcupine poisoning he was tortured by memories of events that had never happened, faces he had never seen. On the other hand, he never sounded as truthful and convincing, never in his lousy soldier's life had he left an impression as strong as that one. Maybe there was something like a Jumping Porcupine of the Universe. It was able to spread its venom to planets, even galaxies, and they got sick of reminiscing for things that never were. Those pictures are chasing them and whole worlds are painfully trying to change something. Maybe we, dogs, meet jumping porcupines in our mothers' wombs and the rest of our days we dream of a world that never existed, remembering a state that never was, fighting for its revival.

Lots of swearing in the room. The soldiers tried everything. They put pillows over their heads, monotonously whistled close to Sever's ear, pinched his nose to force him to breath in a different way. Nothing helped. Now, they were looking for another solution.

Our beds are bunk beds, one can be separated from the other to form normal single beds. Six soldiers were taking up Sever's bed, detaching its frame from the lower bunk. They brought it to the door together with Sever on it. They managed to get it out and leave it in the hall. Nothing disturbed the harmony of Sever's snoring!

Suddenly, Mrako came out of the office and, seeing the

scene, starts to swear. He understood everything, but he had to solve this problem without making it bigger. He woke Sever and told him to go to solitary and sleep there. The bed was better and he would have a room for himself. Everybody, including me, was envious. It was one of those military absurdities. The old soldiers would say, "The worst soldier will do better than the best one!"

I knew that in days that are coming it would not matter who was good or bad.

I turned over on my stomach and fell asleep.

20 BEFORE AXLE-PINNING

Like a sand castle
embraced by waves
the world crumbles.
In foam,
the grains are whirling.
That rhythm
nothing can change.
Days are fading
and days are born
while children play.
The Suns are watching us.
They give us a glory
we must return.

Madness! Andrey had come to the base in the uniform of a control officer! We expected Shaddi. We got information from another base that the helico was coming. Andrey was an axle-pin, the one who penetrates, breaks. No wonder he controlled the situation at the Northern Zone. He found some things that were against Rules and

Regulations. Everybody was stunned by his hurricane of anger. He made soldiers dig trenches in frozen soil. It was about "safe evacuation from our building in a case of artillery attack or air raid." That way we have "the best chance to reach the safety of the forest." Lots of soldiers quietly questioned the tactical purpose of this, because the Arijaans didn't have an air force. They thought it was just a punishment. And it was. When we were alone he told Mrako and me, "The hour of our big attack is approaching! This whole crew must be dead. Everybody! Shaddi might try something. He must have some information. We should not underestimate their abilities. History awaits!"

He raised his palms to the level of his glassy eyes, spreading wide his fingers, "With these hands we will mold the time that is coming! The awakening is about to begin!"

Arijaan troops were supposed to enter the city through our zone. "That is a big honor and responsibility." They should not meet any resistance so the inner rings were never alarmed. The Ring of Lumpens should not be a problem; many of them were already with us. At the top of our axle-pinning formations will be Andrey himself. The purpose was to cut through the city and quickly reach the Core. We got the assignment that was a prerequisite for the success of this offensive. We must show our condor abilities. Shaddi or anything else regarding the Zone was our business.

Andrey did not ask questions. He only delivered answers. He was in command. When he left, we noticed a fly in the office. A fly? Was it possible that it was the same fly the spider killed? Anyways, this one was alive; it was circling around the light bulb just like the helico with a dead pilot. A fly! I saw it as a sign. Mrako was chasing it with no success.

"You heard what Andrey said?"

"Yes."

"We will kill them all?"

"Yes."

"And 'yes' is all you can say?"

"You are a Hallas. And so am I. We have to fulfil our destinies. Nothing can stop us now!"

"Fulfil destiny! We are going to kill 30 dogs and that is nothing to you! You are a Hallas!"

"This is not the time for moralizing."

I didn't show my tears, or my anger. Was it possible that he had no emotions? To kill Finta or Victor, that I could understand, but everybody? Truth be told, all of them were killers, too. They already did it at military high school, practicing war by attacking Arijaan villages, and hunting down escapees, but even then they were just kids pushed by the System to commit a murder.

They had been guarding the Zone for weeks. If you'd never been through that, you had no idea what I was talking about. Nobody understood you. Let's say you were second shift. Not even a soldier from third shift understood. "Shift lasts forever while the weeks fly," soldiers say.

Imagine you were on post One. You guarded from 9 to 11, which meant that at 8:30 you had to go for sentry duty and that you would be back at 11:30. A good corporal who followed the R 'n' R needed 30 minutes to usher one shift in and the other out. First you got shaken and frozen on the helico. It was so cold that even the idea of warmth seemed to be impossible. The benches were on the sides of the cage, that was not good for your kidneys. If the pilot's and corporal's concept of fun was shaking soldiers in the cage they would make sure all your internal organs switched positions. There was a story that pilots used to sleep in the same room with soldiers and that it was changed when one pilot was killed while sleeping. From that time on, legend had it, they always came from the airbase and after six hours took the helico back, when another pilot would take over. Pilots thought that they were the upper crust. Every corporal had to work on diffusing this type of tension.

When he finally got to his spot the guardian thought that everything would be easy now. It was not as cold as it was in the cage. He could walk! But even in the middle of the day, no matter how thick the coat is, he'd freeze his ass off. Those two hours would last and last. He was looking forward to being back at base and hitting the hay. There, he went to the washroom, changed his clothes, washed his hands and face, and maybe his socks, he had a cigarette and it was already noon! Let's say he went to bed. Still, it didn't mean that he could sleep because the commander might get an order to teach classes. Classes? It actually turned into the reading of one of those 'briefings" that discussed "the social and political situation," all of that wrapped in an endless chain of phrases. OK, let's say that none of this happened and the guard really went to bed and really fell asleep. They would wake him up at 13:30 to "prepare" for lunch. Lunch would be at 14:00. Sometimes it would actually be an eatable meal, but most often damned gruel, remnants coming from the kitchen of the closest big camp where 4,000 to 5,000 ate from the same batch. A new guardian would still believe that it was not that bad because he still didn't have to do any work and all of this, even with all that freezing, felt like a vacation compared with the drill. He ate, washed his dishes, and now it was 14:30. In complete combat attire, he walks to the earthwork to receive ammo. Then freezing and shaking in a cage repeat... another two hours of duty and when his time is done, it was 17:00. The same routine again: washroom, washing hands...and if he sleeps the corporal would be waking him up in just 15 to 25 minutes: dinner time! All of them passionately hate the corporal. Some would decide to skip dinner and sleep. In the night ahead they would experience all the sounds an empty stomach can make. Those that ate would not attempt to go to bed because it was almost 19:30, the time of obligatory watching of STANA 1 where they always claim that "the situation in the desert regions is stabilizing." Well, when the show ended, it was 20:00. Some, the smartest, would sleep for 30 minutes. A guard had to use any spare moment to sleep. Possibly, they are just luckier than others: many would not be able to sleep because of their own biology. At 20:30, you know what? Earthwork, a helico arrived, etc. The first night on duty would make everyone shit himself. Not used to the sounds of local fauna, all of them would see bloodthirsty Arijaans hiding in bushes or crawling towards them. When they came back, the guardhouse would look beautiful, like an expensive hotel. There was some good news, they would be able to sleep from 23:30 to 02:30, three hours in one chunk. What a wonderful opportunity! Three of those 10 soldiers would not be that lucky, each of them would have to do one hour of fire picket. You walk in the hall and "protect rifles from being stolen," you meet any sudden visitor and if it was a controlling officer, and it always was, you gave him a report: how many people were in the building, how many rifles, that kind of crap. In general, while on fire picket — you could sit. Your own commander would not punish you for that, but if the control guy caught you, the commander would pretend he never knew anything. When the corporal started yelling around 2:20 everybody would yell back and curse which would not stop an average corporal from threatening and hitting bed frames with his baton. Your stomach was inside out. Frost art was on the windows. The word "shift" sounded like an insult.

"C'mon pussies! Time for the seeeeeecooond shift!"

You came to the earthwork, you still didn't feel cold, actually it felt OK and helped you to wake up, but don't worry: the helico would cool you off. With your palms on your kidneys, you swore that you would kill that pilot. You came to your spot, let's say to One, and since you already felt too cold you immediately went on the watchtower. You didn't give a shit if it was allowed or not. It was warmer. If you were stupid you might want to sit on the floor. It was better to stand and move all the time. But then, since you were bouncing all the time you got tired and you sat... and you fucked yourself up!

You'd be back at 05:15, maybe 5:30.They would immediately pressure you to fix your bed, to clean the room, the hall, the washroom, the classroom, the soc room, to shine your damned boots, clean your rifle and to prepare for the morning line-up. Your commander would do the muster shit, not because he wanted to, but because failure to do so might result in several years of community service in the mining industry. Once in a while, maybe weekly, the control-freak would come to check our rifles.

After that, breakfast. After breakfast, a morning briefing. It was 8:30 and time for another shift. Ask me a stupid question: When do you sleep? The answer is even dumber: you sleep on duty. Day after day, the routine repeated itself. After a while you mastered all the tricks that generations used before you. As soon as you got back you hit the sack without even taking your boots off. Some meals you simply skipped hoping that your friend would grab something for you. Maybe you banked part of a previous meal. Your biological clock was history now, it didn't exist. You slept even at your guarding post, keeping yourself warm in various ways, all of them insufficient. Occasionally, you'd get a bladder infection or something like that and might finally get some rest in the closest medical facility.

They went through all of that, these guys with the dirty underwear, who slept in a room they called "the fart gallery". In a couple of weeks their training would officially end and they would be promoted to the rank of lieutenant, sent to serve somewhere, find a local second-hand girl, get married. Their families would be proud of them.

Mrako always had the ability to read my mind. I thought it was because of some special training, but now I know it was because he loved me.

"You are feeling sorry for those that would throw

Arijaan babies in the air to let them fall on their bayonets!" said he. "Stop thinking! I tell you, I understood something these days. This world IS wrong, including us. But, Andrey is right! We have to attack quickly! If the new breed of defenders gets released, we might run out of options."

"Nothing will ever be the same. What will happen to my parents?"

"I can evacuate them to Bakka Harbour. They would be safe there."

"What do you mean?! You have no power to do something like that!"

"I can call them and set the ransom for your life and tell them to bring me money there. I am sure they would come."

"I doubt it. Father knows everything about Andrey and me. He would never let the Arijaans blackmail him. My dad is gentle, but he won't bend."

"What am I talking about!?" said Mrako. "Every second we are betraying the Revolution!"

"You are wrong. We are not betraying anything. If you want to know, if anybody in all this shit is Hallas, it's us. Not Andrey. He's been looking at Suns for so long that he can't see anything. He's just repeating like a parrot all the words they pressed into his head. And us? Yes, sometimes we're reluctant, but we listen to our hearts."

He embraced me. We kissed for a long, long time, while the raging fly was circling above our heads, drawing in the air a bizarre hello.

21 ICED-OVER RED HOLES

I am sweating underneath my armor. Horses are panting, their back legs lathered. We are speeding through some kind of canyon, more like a passage between giant spruce trees. It feels like a street with tightly-packed skyscrapers. Our horses have no wings yet they gallop through the air, some thirty meters above the ground. The forest is dense, impenetrable. The "canyon" is cut in it by a big mountain river that violently speeds downhill, roaring like a beast, rolling and grinding rocks and trees that submitted to its rage. It doesn't have banks. Tall trees are right on the edge of the river. My hair is long, it waves in the wind. There are three of us and I'm in the middle, leading. My sword points forward. But we are fleeing. The war is lost. It was over.

Our army had been annihilated. We are survivors and we are being chased through the enemy's' land. My palms sweat every time I look at the water that carries the corpses of our soldiers. Many of them, with inflated stomachs, are piling at the edges of this river, a river that feels like a tilted waterfall. We are rushing in panic, whipping our animals, occasionally glancing back to see the chase: warriors in silver armor, with green lizard heads. They are catching up with us.

The mate on my left was constantly whining, "My lord, we'll all die here! I will never see Yovana again!"

Somehow, we think that if the "lizards" catch us, we will be their food. I notice corpses hanging on trees. They are woven into the branches by the long river weed, some with their eyes and mouths open, with rotting faces, some newly dead; some are skeletons in rusty armor!

"The purpose of the chase is not to catch us, but to get us deeper into this trap. It is the mountain that kills! Look at the dead in the trees. They control this river and somehow send a huge wave that smashes armies, runs them into these spruces, or grinds them up by the water stream. Up! We must go up! Up!"

We spur our horses and pull the reigns; we fly high, getting out of this "canyon," above killer-water and killer-forest, bathing in sunshine. I hear angels sing. My body shakes. Somebody grabbed my hand. It was dark. He is calling my name. It was Mrako. What a dream!

In the office, we made coffee. He wanted to leave for Chortville and try to get my parents out. His intention was to make me happy, but I didn't believe he would succeed. Midagar was currently on duty, he was on the helico now.

After an hour Finta was calling from Eight to say that he was surrounded. It would be natural if we sent a unit of soldiers, but we didn't. To Midagar, who just passed duty to me, I said nothing. Instead, I woke up Babic and Lichina, who were stable and confident. When it got tough you want those kinds of people around you. Knowing shrewd Finta's character, I took his information with reservation. I didn't call him, nor did I reply to his calls.

It was absolutely quiet at eight. Jumping porcupines, and nothing else. We didn't even announce ourselves to Finta; we just sneaked out of his land. Back at the base I heard Mrako talking with Midagar in the office. Seemingly relaxed, he was selling him some stupid story. He had to. It was like he talked with Shaddi. Every word that anybody said somehow came back to Shaddi. He didn't even employ hidden microphones. Relying on his network of rats was more efficient and cheaper. Every system that had to extensively use this method was hopelessly rotten. For officers of National Security nobody was clean enough and you never know who the potential enemy was. Their philosophy was that you can find anybody guilty if you are persistent enough. Even if the Revolution fails, this system will keep being wrong. The life of my beloved father stands on this foundation made of lies that are just a fancy cover for prison bars.

I look in the bathroom, nobody was there. I was careful with those things. The walls between stalls were quite high, over two meters, but the ceiling was three. I never thought about that! As soon as I cowered and started peeing something huge fell right in front of me. I instinctively moved and a blade hit the wall close to my head, some plaster went in my eye. I didn't have time to be shocked, that's how fast everything happened. Whatever it was: God, luck, condor training - it helped. I grabbed the attacker's larynx and tore it off his neck. The condor in me triumphed again. The person that was supposed to murder me was Victor, but his expression told me that it was just his shell, not the real him. It was like somebody had him on remote control. I tried to heave the body to the small window below the ceiling, but didn't have enough strength, he was tall and heavy. I locked the door and put the OUT OF ORDER sign on it. I went towards the office to ask Mrako for help and bumped into Captain Shaddi in the middle of the hall.

"Any problems, corporal?"

"Yes, Comrade Captain, there are problems." Mrako was standing at the door, looking at the blood on my hands.

"What the hell is going on!?"

"Victor tried to kill me."

"Victor? Where is he?"

"In the bathroom, Comrade Captain. I killed him."

He jumped in surprise, angry. I opened the door, he leaned over the corpse. Shaddi was red in his face.

"Corporal, you understand that you are under investigation as we speak."

"Serving my people, Comrade Captain!"

"He's not going anywhere!" hissed Mrako from behind, pointing his gun at Shaddi. "Let's chat in the office." The fire picketer in the hall understood that something was wrong, but looked utterly confused.

"It's all in vain!" whispered Shaddi. "I should have killed you long ago, but I thought: Wait a minute; you might catch some bigger pieces using these losers! I guess, I was unlucky, will have to wait for that promotion to major..."

Mrako announced to all the guardians who were on duty that the helico is coming to bring them back to the base. All posts must be evacuated immediately. When the helico came back Mrako had another order for Shaddi.

"Raise the alarm, you sleazy motherfucker, just try not to! Just give me an excuse, please!" Mrako opened the door and pushed Shaddi into the hall.

"Taifoooon!" yelled the wannabe major, Mrako's gun in his back.

The fire picket immediately repeated, "Taiffooon! Taiffooon!"

The usual chaos stormed through the rooms, but in a minute everybody was lined up outside. Some soldiers were wondering out why they didn't get the ammo.

"You should not bitch about that!" yells Mrako, "you will all get your bullets later, don't even doubt it! This alarm is the most special one of your lives."

Mrako commanded them to turn left and then to the right three times and when they had turned their backs to us he ordered them to freeze. Shaddi's teeth chattered.

Mrako looked at me. I understood.

I cut Shaddi's throat and Mrako immediately sprayed the soldiers with automatic gunfire. I did the same. It lasted forever. Some of them almost escaped but we were able to neutralize them. Four of them were still alive moaning in the bloodied snow. Calmly, we checked them up one by one.

I actually felt OK. I didn't feel ashamed of anything. You see, war was misfortune for everybody, even for the winner. It shows you your ugly side, the one you never thought you had. You think: I am this way, but war shows you that you could also be that way and from then on you would have to learn how to live with that. It was good that we didn't think too much because we would probably have screwed up. We let the animals in us take over. We confirmed our lupus ancestry. We are all brought up to be LIKE people, but that's bullshit, a mirage. In war, when all the masks are taken off, you really see who you are. I felt revealed, but only briefly.

He told me that his plan for my family would not work. Father rejected any co-operation with him. One of bodies in the snow moved a bit. We put new cartridges in our rifles and started shooting into the corpses, like killing them once was not enough.

The blood in the snow…

Red icy holes…

What do we do now?

22 THE CEREMONY

Every Hallas knows when the moment of Liberating Strike registers. He does not recognize it by some special signs or omens, but simply feels it in his chest. It is hard to describe that. Maybe it was similar to the state of alert that we might be in when something shocks us. I say "similar," but you can say that only regarding intensity of it. The feeling of a Liberating Strike was long and continuous. A Hallas was never trained nor instructed how to deal with this, but somehow he would know the procedure. He would close his mental doors. At first, he would focus on filtering out all sound information. When he achieved that, when he, for example, could see how two blades hit each other, but he couldn't hear it — then he was ready for the next step. This one was harder. He would work on achieving insensibility to touch so when somebody poked him with a needle or cut his skin, he wouldn't feel anything. Then the sense of scent was eliminated and the Hallas made a mental effort to become blind. When none of his senses worked he would stop breathing.

If he did all of this, he was ready for The Ceremony. Without it any strike would be just a strike and would not merit the adjective "liberating." By closing your gates to the world and life you were able to intensify the process of Diving into Self. How long the period of closing lasts is hard to say. Perception of time is now so different that saying anything sounds ridiculous. Some people think that in terms of real clock time, it did not take less than one second or more than five. Mrako heard that a Hallas who was in the process of feeling Liberating Strike actually physically disappeared, the You-Flesh began to fade until it became totally transparent or non-existent, all your molecules seemingly rearranged. The only thing you would remember was what happened in your dusha,.

Physically, you are falling through the dark space and then you would find yourself high in the sky. It would shape you into your known condor self. The Condor would spread his wings and circle, not thinking of any goal or purpose. Alert, as a condor always is, he would hear a chant coming from below the ground, a chant that rose like dough. And the Condor would think, I must go there! He would dive straight into the ground. Will it mean Death? The Condor was not thinking of it, condor was just doing it, like a plant that moved its leaves in the direction of the sunshine. When it looked that he would hit the ground and break his neck, the Desert would open and he would keep falling and everything would happen over and over.

At the end, he was so exhausted that he could not move his wings. He was far from the world and the affairs of life. Nothing could hurt or disturb him. A mild pinkish light surrounded him like music. He could hear that light. That music was impossible to describe, maybe it was just a single tone. He was holding to it, sticking himself to it, sliding on its invisible plate, letting it lead him back to the Desert, the place of his freedom.

Two suns are setting. It was quiet. Our condor was not alone. Many exhausted condors were landing, turning back into dogs. They sat in the circle and waited, all of them intently looking into one single molecule of air right in the middle, in center, in between them. And when the last trace of light dies beyond the distant mountains, they would see old Aya-Hall. At first he would be a ball of milky light that rotates like planets and stars do. Their eyes would appear to support this hovering and in return it would hypnotize them. Not an eye would blink. The only thing you would hear would be the beating of their hearts. Cacophony at the beginning, but later...

Tu-tururu-tu-tu
Tu-tururu-tu-tu

And when every heart beats like one, the ball would change its shape and they would see Aya-Hall slowly rotating and looking into the eyes of every soldier. Aya-Hall with his scarred forehead, Aya-Hall without his hands, Aya-Hall without his legs, Aya-Hall who under worst tortures that Humans could arrange saw the future for his race, Aya-Hall who shines as a star at the night sky, Aya-Hall who was always around and who was telling them: Freedom! Freedom! Freedom!

Your bone marrow carried the stories of the suffering of your spices. The pain would appear in your stomach and it would explode, illuminating everything that mortals couldn't see: days, years, centuries of humiliation. Years of shame. Neither dog nor Human. Neither Human nor dog. Dog protects. Dog wags his tail, that traditional Canis Vulgaris walking on four legs. And what about us? We didn't walk on all fours, we're not cute, no Human female would ever pet us; we're ugly and short and physically inferior to so-called masters. For ages our genetic code was programmed to fancy two main features: diligence and obedience. We were raised to live with our noses pointed down and even when we would look up it would be with discomfort and fear that we might see the angry face of an owner. That was why we could not see the sky; that was why we could not see birds or clouds! Or stars that blink to hail a night walker!

Once you survived the explosion of pain, you learned something precious: to turn your pain into energy, the strength of the warrior. You would be like those one-cell life forms that live in colonies. You didn't exist without others. You were not possible without other members of the order; they were always with you, even if you never met them or if they are thousands of kilometers away. Every Hallas was your brother, no matter if he was of the monkish kind or from the constellation of the Committee.

When the Bread-Sun
Reaches the spot
And the desert becomes
So hot that it
Burns anything,
A brighter thing
Remains:
My love for you.

23 THEY FIGHT AT NIGHT

They came with the long shadows of the late afternoon. An endless file of worn-out and wounded soldiers, tens of kilometers of continuous marching on their feet. The white bandana around Andrey's head was soaked in blood. They fought at night. They never tried going through the Zone as Andrey claimed. Attacks from the east and south were repelled and both sides suffered heavy losses. Nobody expected that they would go around and attack again.

In Chortville, they were burying their dead and tending their wounded. They must be in panic. If Arijaans entered, there would be no mercy. The city was defending itself with its rings. Many would escape to next inner ring, but that was not possible. Retreating was allowed only when the defense of the currently attacked ring was crushed.

Andrey and his brigade are in a rush. Mrako got new instructions. We needed to stay where we were and with some new, partially disabled soldiers, organize control of Northern Zone. We had to prevent anybody who would try to escape from the city. That included possible Arijaan deserters, too. This surprised me, I'd never expected Andrey to give Mrako such a low-rate assignment, but

Mrako took it with a discipline of the revolutionary.

There was a fire in Andrey's eyes; a fever of his dusha was shaking him. He gave us 30 soldiers, half of them unusable because of their injuries. They were mostly illiterate peasants and shepherds, simple and tough. Deep down, they were probably wondering what's the next hell the city guys would walk them into. Andrey was leaving with his brigade. A piece of his torn and bloody bandana waved in the wind like a flag.

Mrako was giving me instructions. Each shift was now four hours. Some spots would be covered by two soldiers. They looked like homeless people from the city's Lumpen Ring. Unused to cold, they wore night togas, blankets, and all kinds of rugs.

It took a while until Andrey's file disappeared. Then we heard automatic fire. Soon, the ground was shaking and the city where I grew up and which I loved was glowing like a giant bulb in a black desert. One thing I noticed as strange: the system was not using aviation or any armored units. I asked Mrako if I could fly helico for the shift, even as a kid I knew how to navigate it, learned it all playing holo games. He approved. When I came back, he was not there. I had to go to the city. What was going on? Nobody even tried to escape through the Northern Zone!

I entered the lumpen ring, the ring of dog-dogs. A corpse or two here and there, maybe some burnt shack and that was all. Nobody was around. They either all retreated or, which was more realistic, joined Arijaan troops. As I was going deeper the signs of destruction increased and at some point it was hard to distinguish in which ring you are. Thick walls between rings didn't exist anymore. Being only a couple of hours ahead of me Arijaans destroyed so much that I found it hard to believe. Poor dogs must have joined them and that probably multiplied Andrey's brigade. More and more corpses I saw on streets, sometimes whole piles of them. I didn't see any dead Arijaans. Did they pick them up or they are really so superior over defenders? I went towards the tower of smoke that was belly-dancing over the city. I borrowed clothes from a dead civilian and after an hour of intense marching I caught up with Andrey's "troopers."

In the ring of the high middle class revolution was having its big exam. Defense was fiercer, but Arijaans crueler. To ordinary soldiers Andrey allowed everything. They looted, ripped off golden jewelry from ears and noses of captured citizens, they raped. For the very same things a Hallas would be executed on the spot, but a Hallas never does things like that.

I moved a lid on a manhole and descended into sewer, rushing through narrow chutes facing an avalanche of escaping rats. Shaking and detonations were now stronger. I was obviously below the heavily bombed ring of upper-crust dogs. Arijaans were nearing the Core! I listened to my hunch and went up. Couldn't do better — I was in my parents' ring. What I saw would be enough to haunt me for life. There was no resistance. People ran on the street towards the Core in total chaos and confusion. Those that fell down were run over by the stampede. Then, I saw him, a little boy who was fearlessly speeding on his tricycle with plastic helmet on his head and toy rifle on the back. Two seconds later he was splattered all over the wall. Rich dogs were falling down in the rain of bullets. They had no more chances than the wheat facing a combine harvester.

Was this the freedom I dreamed about?

The left wing of our house was destroyed. Our servant Rose was just leaving, dragging a heavy travelling bag.

"Rose, where are Mom and Dad?"

She just looked at me briefly and kept going towards the Core. I caught up with her and slapped her.

"Where are they, you fucking bitch!?!"

"Oh, that is you, Miss Aganovski! I didn't recognize you."

The grenade hit the house of our neighbor, who built his empire selling some hemorrhoid remedy.

"Where they are?"

But Rose had already left, clumsily running on my mother's high heels.

Part of the house that was not knocked down was literally untouched. The audience room was just as neat and spotless as it always was.

"Dad!?"

But father didn't turn back, his silver scruff didn't move. Mother was lying on the couch. They looked like they were resting, but their open motionless eyes told me that they weren't there anymore. The room spinned. For the moment I wanted to join them...pulled myself together and grabbed a pistol from my father's desk, sat in the armchair facing the entrance, accompanied by my dead parents.

I was so tired.

I sat.

I waited.

I didn't cry.

I was hollow.

The right overdose of sedatives finished my parents. My father was killed by his sorrow; my mother was killed by his sorrow, too. Their children were on the other side and dogs like them they called "traitors" and "servants of the Human beast".

Gradually, all the havoc and noise stopped. You could hear occasional begging of those that were to be executed on the street, a scream or two of a raped female. I understood what really happened. No defense was organized. Humans let Arijaans get taste of the battle at the beginning and when they enraged them enough all the crucial troops retreated to the Core leaving population at mercy of vengeful and long oppressed desert dogs. In my opinion, they wanted to unleash the rage of desert dogs and to have them slaughter the city population. That way they would forever discredit the raising myth of a freedom fighter from deserts and keep city dogs more disciplined and better manipulated. When the bloodbath was almost over, "saviors" came! Pompously, Special Forces joined the game: Defenders of the System! Ta-rara-ra! The slaughter of Arijaans had all legitimacy you could imagine, but the real goal was total annihilation of Hallas Order. Defenders of the System were so superior that they quickly turned the score around and blood was now flowing the other way.

It became quiet and dark. It was getting cold. I covered myself with blanket and kept waiting in the armchair. Soon I heard Andrey's steps. When I saw him I realized I was waiting for him all that time. His face was bloody; the sick wide grin showed his white teeth.

"Here is my sister-slut!"

"Did you come to see your parents, you lowlife!"

"Ha ha ha! And you have guts to call ME names!? You, sleazy traitor!"

"Where is Mrako?"

"The People's Court had spoken! Wanna know what it said? Listen!" He raised his gun towards me, slowly, like doing some ritual. That was a mistake. I fired from below the blanket and hit him in his chest. He fell on his knees. With blood springing from his mouth, he still had strength to say, "Different times will come! Different times! And all of you will be sucked into the abyss! Our lives will make sense! The different! Stay damned!"

I made the hole in his forehead and left the house.

24 IT IS COLD

To live uninhibited!? Ha!

Windows were breaking under sudden wave of extremely cold air. At the Institute for Climate Control somebody decided to play with the remaining soldiers of Revolution. I went down into the sewer hoping that warmth of Human bath water, piss, and shit would save me. Surviving Arijaan fighters did the same; it was just an instinct kicking in. Very soon I figured out it was a wrong decision. Everybody outside could see the warm vapor coming from manholes. I thought this was a trap just like the one in my dream about forest of defeat. They would probably pump in some poisonous gas and the business would be done in a clean and efficient way.

I went back to the surface. Why? I guess there was still some desire for life in me, a hope that Mrako is alive.

I was jumping over dead soldiers. Some of them made sounds of crackling ice. The cold was so furious that you lost your breath. I tried to put on myself any piece of clothes I could take from the dead. A broken falus lamp very soon told me that I had come to my destination. I was at the end of my rope, but I finally reached the Morning

Star. I know it was naive, but I did hope that I would find Mrako, the only dog I ever belonged to.

The door was open. It squeaked in the wind. The place was empty. I went down to the dance podium where in the middle sat somebody in a black coat. It was Jester. He looked plain tired of everything, but calm and focused on throwing pieces of broken chairs in the big fire.

"You always come at right time!" said he, not even turning back to look at me.

"How do you know it's me?"

"What a question! How did we ever know to whom to open the door?!"

He had a wrist monitor connected to security cameras. Heat from the fire felt very pleasant. It was life itself. Warmth instantly formed a special bond between us. We could not afford not to be friendly.

"I came to find Mrako."

Jester threw another chair in the fire.

"Would you know anything about him?"

After several seconds of silence he quietly said, "He is dead."

"Where is he?"

"Nowhere. Don't even try to look for him! Seriously, don't you try that! They killed him close to here. Andrey sent a courier to bring him. They arranged a trial. It lasted for about minute and a half. They executed him with a hand rocket launcher."

I didn't say a word.

I didn't cry.

The fire was crackling.

"Sit here and get warm."

"Were we born for this?"

"Don't think too much."

I expected that somebody would wake me up and that all of this was just a bad dream, but the fire was so real.

"Do you think this is the life I hoped for? Leave it alone!

Just look at this fire, how beautiful and always different it is! On the other hand, it would seize if I just throw my coat over it. How about pissing on it in addition, I mean — first you cover it with coat and you piss on it to leave your signature! What do you think about that?"

He was losing it, but I didn't care.

"For me and you, no fire equals dying! We can gamble! We'll throw a coin! Head— we let the fire go, tail — we extinguish it! Correct?!"

I just shrugged. He had thrown a coin. It was head. I am not sure was it for real, but I thought that I saw neighboring intersection on his wrist monitor, streets all in ice and condors falling on the asphalt, with their blood freezing at the very moment it was splashed. They looked just like dead birds now. Those still alive hopelessly tried to go up fluttering like crazy. Soon they would hit the ground. Their feathers were flying around like a snow. Then, Jester moved his hand and I lost interest in watching it. He went to disk-jockey boot and started music.

"Look, you stay here, but I gotta go! There is an invasion of jumping porcupines going on right now and I don't want to miss the show! Yeah, that is something!"

He left.

I stayed.

In a room with roaring speakers.

I'll gnaw your collarbone,
I will not settle for less,
Tonight, I am so alone
Just smile and say, "YES!"

I sat there and let the fire turn out.

I wanted to sleep, to fly through the darkness of universe.

It was true: from a distance, our planet really resembled a jumping porcupine.

25 THE FLIGHT

You glow in my door
With a graveyard smile,
You turn into dust my wine.

Through alien dreams
Like a leaf I fall,
A storm is now my shrine.

On fortress walls:
With my nails, I dig
The tunnel for heart to shine.

At cockcrow
My loss is revealed:
Your moonlight could have been mine.

It's buzzing in my head like it's full of bluebottle flies that have blurred vision and are nervous and eager, randomly laying their eggs, searching for nests for blind pale worms. Tufts of light unveil the darkness. From a flat yellow surface, like icebergs, white lumps stick out. The warmth fills my chest. Schneenockerl! My favorite sweet! But there is no mother to make it! And it is not schneenockerl, but grey clouds that cover everything. On them, black granite rocks float. Am I dead? If I were, that would mean that death is, just like life, a stream of distorted perceptions. I stand on one of those rocks that feel like they shine darkness. Two condors enter the picture.

"You are not dead," says Mrako.

"Your dusha is rambling freely," adds Andrey.

As before, I hear their voices in my head. I would hug Mrako but our anatomies make it impossible.

"That was a precise shot!" says Andrey with a mischievous smile. I just look at him.

"Anyushka, Anyushka!" says Mrako, forget old arguments! Old rules don't apply. Neither Andrey nor I have the will or strength for bickering. Everything was as it had to be."

"And it is peaceful now! We all did what was honorable. I am not angry because you killed me. It's OK now."

We throw ourselves into the sea of grey clouds and fly without a sound.

"So, am I dead or alive?"

"Alive, but your dusha is rambling freely."

"I can see Mom and Dad?"

"Yes, you can. Let's not talk about that now."

"I can meet anybody, dead or alive?"

"Anybody you knew."

"And when I am dead, I will be with you?"

"Probably, if we don't fly into the sun."

"Will you?"

"We don't know. We will do it, but we haven't decided when. That is the most a Hallas can do, but Andrey thinks that we should go back to the layer of the living and enter somebody's soul, so another Hallas is born!"

"Is that how I became a Hallas?"

"We all became one in the same way."

"How come you know everything now? You were also condors before. And I am a condor, too. Why don't I know those things?"

"When you liberate yourself from the flesh, everything simplifies."

"If I were to fly to the Sun right now what would happen to my living body?"

"Nothing. It would just shut down, your heart would stop."

"What if Humans resurrect me and give me assignments?"

"That's impossible. You're something else. They cannot reach you that far. Your corpse would not store any energy. If they attempted to set it on fire it would turn into ash as quick as cigarette paper, but it would not produce the slightest amount of heat."

We are flying up now, leaving grey clouds and landing on an elevating rock. Their gentleness is overtaking me. They remind me of the condor who landed in my window frame in that old dream. Now I know: it was a dead Hallas who came to prepare me for the things that were to come.

"It's so soothing. I'm calm. After all those days that raced by, I'm calm."

"Do you remember the words 'when you lose your mind, you will be born'."

"I do, I do. Tell me, Andrey, how do these rocks float on clouds?"

Mrako smiles and answers instead of Andrey, "How did we come to this world? How does the grass grow? How do we fall in love or become condors? These rocks are our land. There is no doubt that they don't exist for Humans, but neither do we! These are rocks of peace. Their materialization comes as a result of meditation. Remember, you saw them in the cave."

"Why do I see them now?"

"Because you are more with us than in the layer of the living. You just partially share the same reality with them."

"I don't understand. Didn't you say that I was alive?"

"We did. You are still alive."

"But I will not be soon?"

"I guess not!" said Andrey, quietly.

"You guess? Do you know or not?"

"Anya, we don't have to make such efforts. Everything is clear to us. You ask me a question, but you know the answer. It's easy to see that you don't have much desire to be in the Layer of the Living. That's all."

"And you, Mrako, you see the same?"

"Through the same glasses Andrey and I watch. Would you like to fly over the city?"

"Not really. I would like to go to the Northern Zone."

"Why?"

"Why not? Nothing strange in it. My life changed there."

We were diving into a cloud, and then flying under an angle that told me that they didn't have an intention of getting out of it. Before my eyes, the grey vapor was constantly reshaping itself and I recognized the frozen marshlands, the tall trees of number Nine. Everything was still. There were no guards on duty We came to the base. Nobody was around. On the platform, there's a helico with broken rotor blades. We landed at the main entrance. The door was open and the wind had blown lots of snow inside. I didn't feel cold. Next to the rifles, the firewatcher sat and slept. The TV in the classroom was on, but there was nothing on the screen except digital noise. Several plates with the frozen remnants of soup were on the table. On the floor — dice, records of the game are scattered around. I still didn't look in the bedroom, I went to the bathroom. An icicle was sticking out from every faucet, pointy as an Arijaan dagger. Between the trashcan and the wall, my spider friend was patiently weaving his net. Below on the floor an unfinished letter.

"My dear parents, brothers and sisters,

"I've been wanting for a while to at least greet you, and finally I found some time to do so, which was quite a paradox because time was the only thing that we have in abundance here. The only problem is: this time was unusable. I have hours and hours, but I don't have time. I walk with my rifle and I look around. In the beginning, everybody was scared, but you loosen up later, praying that some careless stupid Arijaan bumps into you so you can send him your hello in the form of the bullet. I want to say that I don't believe there would be soon an opportunity for me to come home, except if something like that happens and I get a reward-weekend. You know that I am on guard duty for a while. We protect one of our cities. We are more or less on high alert...

Anyways, we would meet in about two months when I would be lieutenant and get rid of this damn guard. I say all of this so you can say to Boyana not to even try to visit me, for we wouldn't be able to meet. Also, tell her that she will receive a longer letter from me at her address. Please don't send me any money; I have nowhere to spend it. If you are able, send me by Softic some thermo socks and a pair of long johns, but be very careful. If you see that Softic might be willing to bring it to me you will need to give him a bottle of good booze and a smoked pork leg or something like that. If it looks like he's not willing, don't even try, as it might mean lots of trouble for me and maybe even for you. Also, reward with some cigarettes or money the guy who delivers this letter. He is from our province, from Svrakishte, he is a driver and he helped me a lot at the beginning. Don't try to send anything through him, I don't want him to get in trouble. I owe this dog! And, please, also tell Boyana..."

The writing ended there.

"Let's look at the dorm. They must be there," says

Mrako.

"The rifles haven't been cleaned for a long time!" Andrey warned.

We open the door and the stench of stale air hits us. Actually, it's more accurate to say "the stench of soldiers." They all look asleep.

"The sleep of off-duty guards is always heavy and dark," says Andrey.

I laugh. A condor's sense of humor is sometimes strange.

They are all here. Victor Troha lies at the end of the room in the left corner on the upper bed. Taffa is on his stomach, with one leg sticking out of the greasy blanket. Sever is snoring as he always did, but this time he is not bothering anybody. As usual, Stegic is sleep-talking, "That turf, damn! Hand me that turf!" Veseli sleeps as neatly as he lived, he lies on his back, his face a bit to the left, he breathes evenly, sleeps calmly. Ivan Nikolic is unshaved, in a dirty shirt, with a somewhat angry face. When asleep, Ismail looks like an angel. The rest of Zoran Chitkushev is deep, but the face is anxious, he is one of rare soldiers who understands that our world will never be the same. Next to him are Babic and Lichina, one above another, the first one tall and lanky, the second short and portly, both of them healthy and with ruddy faces. Djordjevic, with his long nose, sleeps with a pillow on his head like he wants to send the message that he has no intention of going back on duty. Finta looks like someone who is never asleep, just pretending to be. No need to look for Mefail, his stench quickly told us where he was.

"May your rest be easy, comrades!" I whisper.

For these guys here there will be no line-ups, polishing of boots, cleaning of rifles, taking care not to get caught by control officer while they're sitting or sleeping. Their kidneys will not be shaken by a squeaky helico nor will wind ever chill their bones. None of them will ever scream a greeting so typical of guards: DIEEEEE! That is a replacement for the ordinary hello that contains tears and laughter, desperation and hope, fear, and courage.

"Die!" a soldier will say to a soldier, and usually add something in this style, "My dear poor Stankovic, you will die at One, your bones will rot there! Oh, you fool; can't you see that everybody forgot you! You will piss in your underwear! You have no idea what is waiting for you! You are late, guardian Stankovic! We will always remember you! DIE, GUARDIAN, DIE!"

Those eyes will never see again how frost is conquering the window of the watchtower. There will be no more stolen snacks, cigarettes, washed socks that had no time to dry. Now they are all spared! My friends who will never wake up!

I fought for the army whose only three members I really knew, but served time in the army of our enemies. Those enemies were protecting the world my parents believed in. I loved the dog who was the blood brother of my brother and who was tormented by our relationship. I covered for my brother so he can kill our beloved parents. I wanted to save them, but father's contempt was genuine, painful, and deep. His children spat on everything he did in life! I believed in the revolution, but I betrayed its moral codes. I sympathized with other guards, but together with my beloved Mrako and following Andrey's order I killed them all. Andrey killed Mrako. And I killed Andrey!

"And it's peace now!" reasoned my brother in a gentle voice.

"And everybody's dead!" I added.

"It might be time for you to go," said Mrako. "You have some business to attend to down there."

26 WHAT DO YOU HOPE TO GAIN?

What business had I down there? I understood that when I opened my eyes and saw you. What do you stand to gain? You got my story? Your boss will say kind words? Maybe you'll get promoted and can finally afford that house you are looking at? You're quiet. Just wait and see how quiet you'll become!

Once you sincerely shut up, your problems will begin. You want to know everything! Here it is! Run to your masters and tell them! Stick your tongue out and pant, you might look cute! Whatever you say they'll understand only what fits their needs. Stop writing! Who writes any more, but lunatics who can't fall asleep because they saw a flash of sad eyes in the passing crowd? Listen! Listen and remember! From now on, your life will be tortured by questions. The interrogator in you will turn inward. You watch, but you don't see. The victors are always blind. It is cute that you write everything down and quite strange that you're allowed to do that. I unveiled something to you, but you understood nothing. It is hopeless to open a book before a donkey's eyes. Well, I don't want you to think that I have only insults for you. You are chosen; so am I. You thought that you were questioning me, but I've woven my net around you and you won't get out. You will have to be very strong to carry on. Everything I tell you is yeast and you're the flour and water. The dough of your fear will grow pulling in everything around it: your family, neighbors, co-fucking-workers, city blocks, trains, rivers and mountains, the whole planet.

You will never sleep right again. In the middle of the night you'll wake up covered in sweat, looking for pills. Every bird in the sky will become a condor that waits. You will know that we never lost. Failed revolutions are not doomed, only the successful ones. Victorious revolutions are in real danger for nothing debauches like power. It will feed the one who has it. Since that process ends quickly, in the flesh of the host it will form its own. Through the body of the carrier it will nurture itself. We can barely talk about that person. The flesh of power will eat the host's flesh and he'll have to feed it over and over. He's not his old self anymore! He's someone else, who submissively serves power.

That's why our defeat makes me happy. We accelerated the maturation of our code and got closer to the day when Aya-Hall will let us win. Just think of babies, how they grow up and learn to walk. They take steps and trip, they fall many times. But they also keep trying and in the end they proudly cross the room to conquer the world.

That was why my life is needed. My family wasn't wiped out, nor my love extinguished in a hail of bullets, so that no trace of me remained. When the baby can finally stand straight, the day will come, the day Andrey talked about, the time for everybody to settle their accounts. Now that you know all of this, what have you gained?

You make the world a system of concentric circles, of defensive rings, but for what? You find yourself under the siege of your own illusions. It is not only desert dogs who charge at your city fortresses, but Human misapprehensions coming to take their toll. It is never another who kills us, but our own inability to understand reality. My life suddenly goes in a strange direction. The same might happen to you. You take a shopping bag, step into the street to buy bread and that changes everything! The phone rings! Somebody knocks on your door! You receive a letter or you meet an old buddy and invite him for a drink and the floor opens and — THUMP! You speed down the spiral slide that leads to who knows where. You will live with the feeling that nothing is stable. In your chest you will carry an itch provoked by a dream-breaker. Can you take advantage of that?

Now, you are embedded, caught; only wisdom can save you. The walls are broken. You are a secret passage, a hole in the fortress, an oak door on fire! A million times you will go through my story finding logical flaws and explanations for them, but only to open a bigger puzzle. You will be turning in your bed, feeling the presence of those who are awakening outside the walls. You will know that there is a guard, that misgivings crawl into their hearts, that the cold inhabits their bones, and that some hands, maybe right now, are making the new list of guardians.

When flight is silent
and wings are still,
as you ride the wind
and the desert sighs
its vast dream of grass,
remember old Aya-Hall
who used to say,
"The fish wonders
why water's wet to a Dog.
The Dog's puzzled by the condor
who circles above his master
whose stomach
contains a dead fish.

The master is confused
by the Dog's conduct.
Only the Condor is silent.
Only the condor is free.
He lives by what-must-be."

ACKNOWLEDGEMENTS

My big thanks to poet Colin Carberry who checked and polished my English and skilfully improved translations of several poems that I originally wrote in Serbian, to Urlike Hortian for her thoughtful suggestions, and to poet Fraser Sutherland for his careful copy-editing.

ABOUT THE AUTHOR

Zoran Maslic is an award winning underground filmmaker from Canada. His trilogy In the City of Exile Kings consists of feature-length documentaries When You Die as a Cat, Nobody Knows My Songs, Annoying. They take place in Toronto and follow characters who are restless in their search for their place under the Sun.
Northern Guard is his first book in English. For more info visit

www.exilekings.com

www.ingramcontent.com/pod-product-compliance
Lightning Source LLC
Chambersburg PA
CBHW070042260626
47159CB00005B/2103